Bob Moats

Pasta Murders

By Bob Moats

Copyright © 2014 by Bob Moats.

Rev. 0411141105

Pasta Murders

This book is licensed for your personal use only. This book may not be re-sold or given away to other people. If you would like to share this book with another person, please purchase an additional copy for each recipient. If you're reading this book and did not purchase it, or it was not purchased for your use only, please purchase your own copy. Thank you for respecting the hard work of this author.

This is a work of pure fiction. Names, characters, places, and incidents either are the product of the author's imagination or are used fictitiously, and any resemblance to actual persons, living or dead, business establishments, events, or locales is entirely coincidental.

ISBN – 978-0-9903138-7-8

For information and address:
Magic 1 Productions
P.O. Box 524, Fraser MI 48026-0524
Website: http://murdernovels.com
Cover by Bob Moats

Bob Moats

Other Jim Richards series books by Bob Moats

For a preview or to purchase a book, go to
http://murdernovels.com

What a few people are saying about Murder Novels by Bob Moats

Mr. Moats, I just got your novel "Classmate Murders" and have to let you know, I read it in one evening. That is the first book I have ever done that with. That was the most enjoyable book I have ever read. I just started reading e-books, and reading again, after getting my wife a Kindle. This book was my 12th, and the best. I just got Las Vegas Showgirls to (read) tomorrow evening. I look forward to reading many of your books in this series. I have been searching for an author and books that were fun, entertaining reads. Your books are just the ticket.

Regards, A new fan, Bill from South Carolina

****

Another very nice comment submitted through my website from Micki P.:

"I recently was given a kindle for my 60th birthday. The first book I downloaded was the Classmate Murders and have now read every one of the them. Today I started on the Fatal Rejection series. Thank you for the wonderful ride with Jim and Penny and all the rest of the troop. I have laughed and giggled thru the stories, my poor family gave me the strangest looks! Now I really want a little Yorkie!! Fatal Rejection so far is another great read! I will be looking out for more of Jim Richards and since you are my #1 Author, anything of yours I can find."

Extra special thanks to:

Special thanks to Val Brooks who edited this book and for her great suggestions.

Thank you to all the people who purchased this book. I hope you enjoy it as much as I enjoyed writing it for my faithful readers.

The Jim Richards Family of Readers is listed in the back of the book.

Pasta Murders by Bob Moats

Chapter 1

Angelo.

That name struck fear in the hearts of men who didn't pay their gambling debts on time to the Traviano mob family in New York. The mention of his name and the threat of a visit from him would make strong men cringe in fear. Angelo never actually touched anyone. He had men to do that. It was his job to see that people paid up or walked funny.

Angelo was brought up by his mother, Francis, the matriarch of the family. Ever since she was a young woman, she had been married to mob capos, two of whom died at the hands of rival gangs. Her newest husband, don Gino Traviano, ruled the illegal gambling operations in his territory and took on his stepson to enforce the rules he set down as to delinquent payments.

Angelo was actually a kind person, but he had an image to uphold. He wouldn't let anyone get out of paying.

Today, Angelo held a meat cleaver high over his head. He brought it down with such force that the blade cut cleanly through the flesh and bone. He grinned as he separated the meat and made a few more whacks.

Angelo was preparing steaks to be eaten in his new restaurant that he recently opened in Las Vegas. He had turned his back on being a leg-breaker for the family and, with his mother's and stepfather's blessing, moved from New York to Las Vegas. He first started working for Richards Investigation and Security as a celebrity bodyguard, then Jim Richards made him an offer he couldn't refuse. Jim fronted the money so Angelo could open his new restaurant, one he had wanted for a long time.

Angelo was preparing a special dish for a distinguished visitor to his newly opened establishment. A food critic from the Las Vegas Review-Journal newspaper was coming in to check out the place. Most the time this food critic wouldn't announce that he was coming, but Angelo had an inside with all the right people through his past connections to the mob. He got word the reviewer was coming, so he worked hard to make sure his visit was the best.

Little did Angelo know that the critic's meal in his restaurant would be his last.

~~*~~

It was a Saturday morning and I stood outside the Victoria's Secret store in the Boulevard Mall waiting for Penny to come out. She went in to buy a new bra she saw advertised on TV last night. She just had to have it. The ad promised that the bra would make her breasts pop out even more. But she didn't need much help in that department. She was well built.

Even though she was sixty, she still had a nice firm body, and her breasts still stayed north of her belly button. But she had to have this bra, so I endured going shopping with her, a job I never cared for.

I went to the benches they provided for weary husbands to relax while the wives spent their money. I didn't worry about money. I made enough from my book sales and from my investigations of husbands going wild. The detective work was doing well and, with Will Trapper and Earl Daws, it was actually fun. Buck had his security team of around 180 men. He was happy.

Life was good in the Vegas valley. Tourists were starting to flock in as the economy got better. I didn't have any more murders to investigate since the fashion show models were killed. I actually had a small respite since that case. Penny and I did a lot of exploring around the area, going camping a couple times on Mt. Charleston. Of course the motorhome van I owned was like living in a motel, so the word camping was not really descriptive of what we did.

"You're not supposed to be resting," came a voice to my right. It was Penny with bags in hand. She sat next to me and started to open the top bag. I had a feeling she was going to pull out the bra to show me. I didn't need that in public.

I reached over, put my hand on the bag and said, "You can show me later, even model it for me."

"If you're lucky," she replied closing the bag. "Have you been sitting here all the time I was in the store?"

"No, I begged for coins from the tourists to pay for your purchases."

"You know very well I pay with my own money. I have more than you do."

"I've never snooped in your checkbook to see, but I think we're both well off."

"I remember when you were poor and struggling," she said with a smile.

"I was temporarily unemployed when we ran into each other again."

"Ran into each other again? We had sex on the floor of my dressing room in Michigan. It wasn't half bad."

"Yeah, you were adequate, as I remember. But you're getting better."

"You're never going to see me in this bra," she said and stuck her tongue out.

"I'll sneak it out of your dresser and try it on."

"You do, and you'll stretch it out, so keep your hands off. I'm hungry."

"Shall we go to the food court and get something?" I asked.

"Fine with me, you're paying." She stood and waited for me.

"Oh, now I pay. What happened to all your money?"

"I'm saving it for more bras." She laughed and headed toward the food court. I got up as fast as my body would let me and followed.

Pasta Murders

We had our meal and then left the mall, heading back home. Our faithful toy Yorkie, Willy, rested on Penny's lap. He stayed in the van as we shopped. He didn't mind, and the van was big enough for him to run around. It was a Class B motorhome, built on a van body so it looked small, but inside it had a kitchen, bath, bedroom and everything in between. I had always wanted one, and bought this one while Penny and I were in Florida on my book signing tour.

I pulled into the drive and parked on the side of the garage. I had my restored 1989 Crown Vic next to my mini limo in the garage along with Penny's car, so the van stayed outside. We went into the house, and I shut off the driveway alarms and reset them. The house was on the western edge of Las Vegas and overlooked the Valley with the Vegas strip in the distance providing a beautiful view.

It was quiet in the house. Angelo had been staying in our guesthouse since he moved to Vegas, but he left just after he opened his restaurant. He wanted a place closer to his business. We missed him and all the great meals he cooked for us, especially the breakfasts. I knew he wanted a restaurant, so I offered to front the money for it, and he agreed.

It had been open about a month, and the business was doing quite well. I think his mob connections helped, and he had a number of local family members dining there now. He didn't want the place to become a hangout for the mobs, but they all respected Angelo and didn't make a fuss while they were there.

I just wanted to be sure no rival mobs rolled in and shot up the place to do a hit on some mob capo.

Bob Moats

My cell phone buzzed. The caller ID said it was Trapper. "Yeah, chief, what do you want?"

"Just checking in. It's been too quiet around the office this last week. Lacey and Mac went on vacation, and Tracey is having fits trying to make heads or tails of Lacey's file system. That's the most excitement we've had. You've been hiding out. I wondered if you were going to work anymore."

"I plan on coming back in. The weather has been so nice, Penny and I have been running around checking out all the sights we haven't seen since we moved here. Have you been to the new mob museum yet?"

Trapper laughed and said, "No, I had enough of that stuff when I was a boy here in Vegas. I remember my dad talking about the gangsters who were running the town back in the fifties. I don't need to be reminded."

"So what's Earl doing?" I asked.

"Haven't seen much of him. He took a case for some company to find out who's leaking company secrets."

"Ah, industrial espionage, right up his alley," I said.

"Yep. I'll let you go. Will I see you Monday in the office?"

"I'll make an effort to put in an appearance. Talk then," I said and hung up.

"Who was that?" Penny asked as she came into the living room. She sat next to me on the couch and handed me a beer.

"Ah, you know the way to my heart," I said as I popped the top. "That was Will. He's bored and wanted to know if I was, too."

"Well, are you?"

"Around you, I'm never bored. What do you have cooked up for tomorrow?"

"I thought we'd go to church. It is Sunday," she said with a slight smile.

I just stared at her until she laughed. "Sorry, I couldn't resist."

"It's not that I'm against religion, but there are too many out there to choose from."

"You could start your own. You are an ordained minister from that online church."

Before I could say anything in response, my cell phone buzzed again. It was Angelo. "Hey, friend, what's up?"

"How'd you and the Mrs. like a free meal? I need people in my place to fill seats. Got a special customer coming in tonight."

*

Chapter 2

"Must be something special if you're filling seats," I said.

"It's the restaurant critic from the R-J. He can make or break a restaurant with just a word. Even the tour books take his word seriously. I'm having fits getting ready for this. I need your calming effect."

"Well, I'll be there, and I'm sure Penny will be happy to eat out again. What time do you need us?"

"I understand he'll be here around nine. So if you could fill the seats till he gets here, it would be great."

"Okay, my friend, we'll be there around eight-thirty. Talk later," I said and hung up.

"Where are you having me go?" Penny asked.

"Angelo invited us to dinner at Momma Mia. It's free. So I hope you'll go."

"Anything for Angelo. What's the special occasion I heard you mention?"

"He has a food critic from the R-J coming and wants the place to have customers. Shall I call Deacon and Lynn?"

"I think they'd like that. We haven't seen them in a while, crime has been so quiet. Let's invite Will and Samantha and also Earl and Paula. Make it a party." Penny was bouncing on the couch now.

"You should go into the party planning business. I'll call all of them and see if they're available. I should warn Angelo to have a big table ready." I went to my writing desk in my work room for a little privacy and called everyone. Amazingly, everyone was available. I called Angelo, and he was delighted that I was bringing so many people. I insisted that I pay for the others. He tried to argue, but I won. I hung up and sat back, looking at Willy sitting on the floor by my desk. "I'll bring you home a doggy bag."

Everyone had assembled at our house by eight and was chatting about the dinner. I gathered them all up, and we drove out to the restaurant on Flamingo Avenue. Angelo had valet parking this evening, so I gave the keys to the man and he drove Penny's car off. I watched it go, thinking about the last car she had. It was falling apart, so I got this new one for her sixtieth birthday.

Angelo was dressed to the nines in his tuxedo. He stood by the door greeting customers and taking them to their seats. He saw us coming and gave me a big smile.

"Angelo, where's your hostess, the cute blond?" I asked.

"I wanted it to be a personal touch tonight, so here I am." His smile was infectious. His grammar had improved greatly over the year he'd been out here. When I first met him, he sounded like a gangster from the old movies, but he constantly worked on improving his verbal skills.

"Well, I hope it works out for you. I brought the whole gang, so you can seat us."

He led us to a big table in the middle. I could hear people speaking quietly about seeing Penny. She was the host of a local talk show. Before we moved to Vegas her show had been national on the CW network. She quit the national show, but after we arrived here, the local TV station talked her into hosting their show. Everywhere she went her fans ogled her.

"Angelo, maybe I could do a show from here one day. With a segment on cooking genuine Italian delicacies?"

"I'd like that Mrs. R, that would be nice." He beamed. He saw more people coming in and excused himself.

"I love what Angelo has done with this place," Lynn said as we sat.

"It was a dump before he got it," Deacon said.

Lynn was looking more pregnant and more uncomfortable. I asked, "How are you feeling Lynn?"

"Miserable but happy. Our sonogram says it's going to be a girl. We just found out yesterday."

Everybody was cheering and congratulating her and Deacon. I sat thinking back to the time I first met Deacon when he was protecting Penny from the classmate killers. Then I thought about how he fell in love with Lynn when we met her during the Showgirl murders here in Vegas. Seems all our good moments involved murder.

The waitress was at our table in short order and handed out the menus. Most of us already knew what we wanted, having eaten there before. She took our drink orders and left.

"So, Lynn, are you on a desk or still investigating crime?" I asked.

"Captain Weber forced me to sit out crime. Hell, I'm a homicide Lieutenant, I should be investigating."

"You know you're needed, but not in this condition," Deacon said. "You can sit it out for the next few months, until the baby is born."

"Then you'll need a baby sitter," Earl said.

"God, I forgot about that. I can't stay at home all the time. I need my crime fighting," she said with a moan.

Earl's girlfriend, Paula spoke up. "Lynn, I'd be more than happy to watch the child. I had one baby of my own before she grew up and left home."

Pasta Murders

"Paula, that's nice of you. I'll keep it in mind."

Trapper said, "Deacon, are you still in homicide or did they move you back to Vice?"

"I'm still in homicide. Weber decided I was needed there more than in Vice. After the fashion show killings he decided to let me stay. I miss the hookers, but duty calls."

Lynn hit him on the arm and then made a noise. "Sorry, it's the baby pushing on my internals. I hope I can survive the evening."

Our drinks came and we relaxed. "Where's Buck?" Trapper asked.

"He's busy with his security team. Too many guards copping out of work. He has to fill in during their absence," I replied.

Trapper laughed. "I remember years back when I was chasing Buck on the streets of our city back in Michigan. He was a bad boy, and I was the cop who wanted to take him down. Glad to see he's doing better now."

"He's still a bad boy, but more refined now," I said.

Angelo came back to our table. "Listen guys, I want to thank you for coming in. I just wanted to be sure to have customers when this critic comes in. It's important for my business."

"Angelo, anything for you," Trapper said.

"That's how all of us feel," Earl said.

I was happy with the men I associated with. They were good people and good friends. This was a journey of three years since I first started in my P.I. business. They made it better.

16

"Oh, crap, he's here," Angelo said, his gaze focused on the front entrance.

He rushed off and greeted the man, trying to act like he didn't know who he was. He had warned all of his servers to pretend not to know the man. He didn't want the critic to know he was expected.

"Yes, sir, dining alone?" he asked the man.

"Does it look like I'm with anyone?" The critic spoke with a snarl.

"Sorry, sir, I just wondered if you'd be joined by anyone," Angelo replied.

"No, I'm not being joined by anyone. Now can I have a seat, or do you want to stand here all night?" he sniped.

Angelo was beginning to think this guy wasn't so nice. He took him to a table off to the side, fairly private but still in the way of seeing the entire room.

"I'll have a waitress here shortly, sir." He signaled the girl, and she came over.

"Evening, sir. Would you like something from the bar?" she asked and handed him the menu.

"Do I look like I need a drink?" he snapped.

"No, sir. May I suggest the Beef Roast Marinara?"

"I'll have the Beef Stroganoff. And no more prattle. I'll have a dry martini with a twist. Can you handle that?"

Pasta Murders

"Yes, sir, I can, thank you." She went off trying to hold her tongue.

She burst into the kitchen where Angelo waited for her. "That man is a pig!" she burst out. "I want to spit in his Beef Stroganoff. Angelo, can I spit in his food?"

"No, Cathy, you can't, but if he is really a pig, I'll take care of him." Angelo went out of the kitchen as the girl placed the food order then went to get the pig's martini.

She took the martini to him and waited as he tasted it. "My God, doesn't your bartender know how to make a decent Martini?" he spit out the words.

"I'm sorry, sir," she said. Angelo heard and came over.

"Sir, if the drink isn't to your liking, I can get you another," Angelo said trying to soothe the man.

"I certainly hope I'm not being charged for this bilge water."

"No, sir, it's on the house, and all your drinks will be, also." Angelo was trying not to revert back to his leg-breaker days. He wanted to take this man out back and crush his vocal cords.

"Very well, have a good drink brought to me, now," the critic ordered.

Angelo told the waitress to fix the drink, then he walked away.

"Are all critics assholes?" Angelo asked me as he came up.

18

"I've found that many book critics can be assholes. But there are a lot of good ones too," I replied.

"Well, this one isn't very nice. He has a chip on his shoulder, or he's just a jerk to begin with."

"Has he ever given a good review?" I asked.

"To tell you the truth, I don't know. He must, as he is a big man around the restaurant circles. I've asked, and they all tell me his word is important. But if he keeps being a jerk I may not be able to keep my temper."

*

Chapter 3

"Well, hang in there, Angelo, he may be just trying to see if he can rile you. Keep a cool head, and he might end up liking the friendly people here," I said, hoping to ease him into relaxing.

"Yeah, that's true. Maybe he's seeing if we would be assholes, too," he said with a big grin.

"Very true, now go be a good host. Let him see you care for your customers."

"You got it, Mr. R. I'm glad you're here," he said and went off.

I turned to Penny who was listening in on our conversation. She said, "I hope this critic is just doing his best to see how far the staff can be pushed and not lose their temper."

"I hope so, too. I've never heard of this guy. I guess, from what Angelo said, he is respected for his opinions. I hope he has good things to say about Momma Mia."

I pulled out my new Android smart phone to check something. I had always been a big supporter of Palm devices, but they were fading from the scene. The Android phones were great for all the apps and features they had. I bought the new Samsung Galaxy Note and, even though it was huge, it packed a wallop for features. I opened up the Google search feature and went to do a search on this critic. I realized that I didn't even know his name. I did a search for the food critic for the Las Vegas Review-Journal, and the browser came up with him and his picture. I was impressed.

The man's name was Alfred Horn. He had been a critic for many newspapers before settling into Las Vegas. This city has an overabundance of restaurants, so he was in his element. There were several articles that told about his abusive nature and how he was instrumental in closing down a number of restaurants. That made me worry.

I scrolled down the Google webpage, reading more about the man. Trapper leaned over next to me to see what I was up to.

"I'm checking out this critic. Name's Alfred Horn, and he can be a bastard, judging from comments I've read," I said as I showed Trapper my tablet phone.

"I heard what Angelo had to say about him. I hope he does stay cool," Trapper replied.

"Well, we need to keep an eye on Angelo, just to be sure. Don't want him leg-breaking Horn. That wouldn't do well for the restaurant."

"Or for Angelo," Trapper added, and I agreed.

Our food arrived, and everyone started in on the meal. It was as delicious as it was the first time Penny and I ate there. Angelo did a lot of the cooking, but he had trained a couple other cooks to do as well. We were all enjoying our food quietly as I kept an eye on Horn sitting at his table eating his food.

He didn't look displeased, but he wasn't smiling either. Angelo would walk by every so often to see if he needed anything. I noticed that Horn switched to wine. Angelo had his wine steward serve him the beverage. At least they couldn't screw up that drink.

Horn finished his meal, took out a small notebook and began to write in it. I saw Angelo standing off to the side watching the critic. He looked worried.

Horn stopped the waitress and said something, probably wanted the bill. Most critics won't eat a meal for free and will even turn down the offer. It was something that they couldn't do. It would look like getting a favor for a good review. The waitress brought back the tray with the bill and set it on the table. He looked at the bill and just sat back.

I wondered what he was doing.

Pasta Murders

Angelo was to the point of worrying that the evening for the critic hadn't gone well. He stood a while watching the man. After he received his bill he just sat unmoving. Angelo figured he couldn't make the evening any worse so he went to the table again.

"How was your dinner, sir?" he asked the man.

"Mr. DeMarko, I understand you were an enforcer for the mob," he said briskly.

"I was, but that is in the past now."

"How did you end up running a restaurant? Mob business slow?"

"No, sir, I just didn't want that life anymore. A good friend of mine offered to help me get this establishment going, and I took his offer. I've always wanted a restaurant."

"You have many mob associates dining here now?" he asked with a smirk.

Angelo bit his lip, trying to keep his head. "None that I invite. If a customer comes here to eat, I let them, no matter who they are."

"Noble. I hope it doesn't become a gathering place for the criminal element."

"Well, it's not something I would allow. This is a nice family restaurant, and not *family* as in mob. Parents can bring their children and relatives to eat here without worry."

Horn sat staring at Angelo, then said, "I'll have another glass of wine if you have nothing better to do."

"Right away," Angelo said and went off to get the wine steward.

~~*~~

Penny was having me explain what was going on. I told her about the find on Horn from Google. She looked at the phone and read a bit.

"I think this calls for a little help from a celebrity." She stood, took my hand and tugged me to my feet. I worried about what she was up to. She walked around the room, pulling me behind her, and came by the table where Horn was sitting. She started to walk past but stopped. I nearly ran into her.

"Excuse me, but aren't you Alfred Horn?" she asked the man.

He blinked and looked a little shocked. "Yes, I am. You are Penny Wickens, aren't you?"

"Why, yes, I am, and this is my husband Jim Richards. I've read your column and enjoy your perspective on good eateries. You must do a lot of exercising to keep the weight off from all that food."

He didn't smile but nodded. "I do keep in shape, yes."

Penny leaned closer. "Are you doing a piece on this restaurant?"

"I'm thinking about it. I like to dine first, then form opinions. Do you dine here often?"

"Yes, it's our favorite restaurant. Angelo is a close friend to us, and Jim helped to open his business."

"Ah, I see, so you are prejudiced towards his success. Is that it?"

"Well, we'd like to see him succeed, yes. Angelo worked hard to start this restaurant."

Pasta Murders

"I'm sure you'd do anything to help him."

"Well, of course," she said, wondering where he was going with this.

"So you're trying to butter me up, hoping for a good review. I appreciate that you are a celebrity around Vegas with your cute little fluff show, but I don't appreciate being stroked. Now, if you'll excuse me, I want to enjoy my wine before I leave."

I've rarely seen Penny without words, but she stood there staring at Horn for several moments before she finally spoke. "Excuse me for bothering you, Mr. Horn. I can be sociable without motive. Excuse me now while I go far away from your table."

She nearly yanked my arm off my shoulder as she stormed away. We went down the hallway to the restrooms, and she stopped.

"That man is an asshole! Insufferable twit! I want Angelo to break his legs then his neck." She was furious. Penny rarely gets furious. I wanted to get away, but she was still squeezing my hand.

Angelo came around the corner and asked what happened. Penny told him, and he frowned.

Penny calmed and said, "I wasn't trying to start anything. I just thought if I could put in a good word it might help."

"Mrs. R, that was real nice of you. I think this man wouldn't be happy no matter what. I just may throw him out anyway and say, damn the review."

I pulled my hand from Penny's and held on to his arm. "Let it go, Angelo, let him leave on his own steam and see what happens. Horn underestimates the power of Penny Wickens. She has friends in high places. Horn will regret pissing her off."

Angelo laughed for the first time that night. It sounded good. "Yeah, I'll let him leave on his own, but he's never allowed back in here if he can't be civil."

We returned to the dining room, and Penny led me back to our table. Everyone asked what was going on so Penny explained what happened.

Deacon said, "You want I should arrest him for loitering? He's still sitting there."

"No, I told Angelo to just let him leave and see what happens. It's better than really pissing him off."

"True, but it would be more fun to arrest him," Deacon said with a grin.

"I never trusted food critics," Lynn said. "Who's to say his palate is any better than mine or yours? And does he hate burgers and fries? How's that for snobbery?"

Earl said, "I could call my friend Harold in the bureau and have him run a background check on Horn. Maybe we could find some black eye to embarrass him with."

"Let it go. This restaurant will survive on word alone, plus I may have a couple billboards put up around town," I said, with a smile.

"You sure want to protect your investment in this restaurant," Trapper said.

"Damn right. Angelo and I both have a stake in this place."

Earl pointed to Horn, and we looked over just as he was getting up to leave. "Good riddance," I said.

Chapter 4

"Can I follow him out and beat him up?" Penny asked.

I laughed and leaned over to kiss her cheek. "No, my love, you may not. I know you could, but it's better to let him go. And hope he doesn't write a bad review for Angelo. I don't know how he would react."

"Maybe bring in the family to pay a visit to Horn," she said with a smirk.

"That's a thought, but not now. We need to finish the meal and go home," I said and turned back to my Chicken Primavera.

"Boy, you are getting to be a poop in your old age."

I laughed again. "Eat your food and save what you don't eat for Willy."

"What?" Trapper said.

"Not you, Will. I was talking about our dog Willy."

"I remember when you named him after me, I was not pleased. But the dog is all right. So I'm good with it now."

We finished the dinner as Angelo came over to see how we were doing. "Everything is very good, my friend. You have a five star restaurant, and I'll buy up all the taxi tops in Vegas to advertise your place," I said referring to the small billboards they had on the top of taxis.

26

Bob Moats

Angelo laughed and said, "That would be nice as long as you don't put my mug on the signs."

"Would your mother mind if we used her image?" I asked.

"I'll check with her, but as a member of a New York crime family, I wouldn't count on it."

"Well, we'll need a picture of a nice Italian woman cooking at a stone stove. Maybe the family standing behind her with plates in hand waiting for the goodies she's creating."

"You do what you think is good. I trust you."

"Thanks, Angelo. Now we're finished, and your critic's gone. So are you all right with his visit now?"

"Not much I can do. I gave up threatening people to make them do things they didn't like. I am a business man now and need to remember that."

"Good for you. Send Lonnie over with the bill, and don't argue. I'm paying for this motley group. You may as well make some money tonight."

Angelo smiled and went off to find our waitress. I looked at everyone as they gathered money to leave a tip. They plopped down a large pile of cash on the table.

"Are you guys paying for Lonnie's college education?" I asked.

"We're good people and value good service," Earl said.

"I'm sure Lonnie won't forget us when we come back," I said as she came over to give me the bill. She eyed the tip money and cracked a small smile.

I took out my debit card and put it on the tray with the bill. She picked up the tray and left again.

Pasta Murders

"So shall we go dancing now?" Lynn asked.

"You've got to be kidding. You're about 10 weeks from delivering a huge baby girl, if she's anything like Deacon. You want to go dancing?" Penny said.

"I need the exercise. It's good for the baby," she replied.

I looked at Penny. She smiled and said, "Looks like you don't go home now."

"Poor Willy, he'll be so hurt," I replied. I turned my gaze to Lynn and asked, "So where do you want to go to dance?"

"The MGM Grand has that club where the band plays easy listening music. Easy enough for me to handle."

Everyone nodded their approval.

"Okay," I said. "I guess we go there."

We all stood, and I asked Angelo to stop by our home when the restaurant was closed. I wanted to talk to him.

"Sure, Mr. R, I'll be out of here by midnight. Is that too late?" he asked.

"No, I'll be up," I said as everyone was heading to the door. Lonnie gave me back my debit card and the receipt, then started to clean the table. She scarfed up the tip real quick. I smiled and followed my friends.

We ended up at the MGM Grand and had a nice time boogying for a couple hours. Lynn was wearing down, and Deacon took her home. Earl and Trapper took their ladies off leaving Penny and me sitting at the table. The room was busy, people enjoying themselves, back from gambling, drinking and now enjoying the music.

"I had a good time tonight," Penny said. "I hope it all works out for Angelo."

"I invited him to the house tonight. I want to discuss advertising to head off Horn and his review. I'll plaster Vegas with Momma Mia, so it will be hard not to see a billboard or taxi top that doesn't scream out the restaurant."

Penny smiled and took my hand. It was a slow dance, a Shania Twain song, one we first danced to when we married here in Vegas. She held on tight, as if she was afraid I'd disappear. We move slowly around the dance floor. It was no longer crowded. The song ended, and we went back to the table, but I didn't sit.

"Let's go. Willy will think we deserted him." We went out to our car in the parking structure and drove away.

The night was cool, not hot like it usually was in the valley. During the day it would get up to a hundred plus degrees, but it was dry so you wouldn't suffer too badly. Most of the time we were in air conditioning, but would often venture out to do our business.

We pulled around the last curve towards our home when I saw Angelo's car in our drive. I pulled in next to him, hit the remote opener, and drove into the garage. Penny and I went over to Angelo as he got out of his car.

"You're early," I said looking at my watch. It was only eleven fifteen.

Pasta Murders

"I had to get away from the place. I was so frustrated by the disaster tonight, I had to get away. I hope you don't mind," he said quietly.

"Angelo, you're our friend. We will always be there for you. Let's get in the house so I can turn off the driveway alarm before Willy goes nuts."

We went in and Willy bounced around Angelo's legs. "He misses you since you left," I said as I reset the alarms.

"I'll be sure to visit often then." He smiled.

"Let's go in the family room and relax. Would you like a beer?" I asked.

"After this night, I'd like that, yes," he replied.

I took out three beers from the fridge and opened them. I gave one to Penny and one to Angelo.

Penny and I sat on the couch with Angelo on the easy chair in front of us. "You said something about advertising?" he asked.

"Yeah, we need to do a full blown attack on the public. You've seen the billboards for Richards Investigations and Security with Buck and me looking tough."

Penny laughed. I looked at her. "Yes, and those billboards have brought in business, or I would have pulled them long ago."

She gave me a smile and remained quiet.

I continued, "Now we need to talk to the company that takes care of the billboards and taxi tops and get a campaign started."

"I appreciate this, Mr. R. I'll help however you need."

"Good, so let's talk about how we're going to set this up."

We talked long into the night. I brought out a drawing pad, and we sketched some ideas for the signs. We went through a number of hours and a number of beers before we tired out.

"Angelo, you're not driving home tonight after all this beer. Go back to the guestroom and crash," I said, and he agreed. He had scarfed down a lot of beer to relieve his tension from the evening.

He went off to the guesthouse, followed by Willy. We let the dog go with him. He had slept with Angelo before, so we knew he was all right. Penny and I sat on the couch and kissed a while.

"You're a nice person. I think I'll keep you," Penny said to me.

We went to bed and didn't even fool around, we were both so tired. Penny was immediately out and snoring softly, less than she usually did. I couldn't sleep, which was no surprise. I usually couldn't go to sleep right away, and then I would wake early, not able to get back to sleep. They say as you get older you need less sleep, but that didn't help my disposition. I enjoyed my sleep, other than the dreams that had me working for past employers that I hated.

It was quiet in the house. Angelo was back in the guesthouse, Willy sleeping with him. I was sure they were both happy. I was at a good time in my life. I had money from the sales of my books and from my detective business so I could enjoy spending it on things like restaurants and advertising. What else would I spend my money on? I couldn't take it with me, so I might as well use it.

Penny turned over and said, "Go to sleep. I can't sleep if you are awake." Then she went back to sleep. She was an amazing woman. Loving, kind and wanting to do good things. I was so lucky to have her.

I finally fell asleep.

Morning came quickly. I woke to find Penny was off to her private bathroom doing whatever she does to look great. I got up and went to my bathroom. It needed cleaning. I knew I had to stop one day and clean it.

Willy came running into my bathroom just as my cell phone buzzed. I said, "How did you get back in? Did Angelo leave you?" I looked at the caller ID. It was Angelo.

"Angelo, you must have left early."

"I did, Mr. R, but I got a problem. I came to the restaurant and opened up." He paused. I waited. "I need you to come down here. I found Alfred Horn in my dining room, dead, with his head in a plate full of spaghetti."

*

Chapter 5

"Don't touch anything, and don't let your employees in. I'll call Deacon and Lynn and get them to head this off. Be cool and stay away from the body. Better yet, stay outside until we get there."

He said he would, and I hung up. I speed dialed Deacon. I could tell he was still sleeping. It was Sunday morning, and he didn't work on Sundays.

"This better be good," he said.

"It's Jim. Angelo went to this restaurant this morning and found Alfred Horn dead in his dining room."

I could hear Deacon choking and clearing his throat. "What?" he finally said.

I repeated myself, and he was silent for several moments. "I'll tell Lynn and we'll be there shortly. He hasn't called 911, has he?"

"I don't think so. He called me."

"Good, I don't want anyone else to grab this case. Call and warn him to wait for us."

"I will," I said and hung up then called Angelo back.

"Deacon and Lynn will be out shortly. I'll be there, too. Don't call 911 or anyone, just wait outside and keep people away."

He said he would and hung up.

I finished in the bathroom and dressed. Penny came in and could tell something was wrong. I told her, and she finished dressing, also.

We drove in the van and arrived at the restaurant about twenty minutes later. Angelo was standing outside with a couple of his employees. Deacon and Lynn pulled in right behind us.

"Tell me what happened," Lynn said to Angelo.

"I came in early to get the kitchen set up, and I saw the lights in the dining room were on. I left early last night and told the staff to shut everything off. I was not happy that they left the lights on, so I went in to turn them off until we opened. When I went into the dining room to shut the lights down, that's when I saw him."

"Alfred Horn?"

He nodded. "I didn't know it was him at first. I went to him and looked carefully, not touching him, and I could see his face in the spaghetti. It was Horn. I called Mr. R and told him, and he called you."

"Good, stick to that story. How could he get in here after hours and where did you go after you left last night?" Lynn asked.

"I have no idea how he got in unless someone let him in. I left here last night and went straight to Mr. R's house and was there all night."

Lynn looked at me. "Is that true?"

"Yes, we talked about advertising for the restaurant until two in the morning. Angelo was drinking beer with us, and I didn't want him to drive, so he stayed in the guest house."

"Okay, we need the ME, Joe Lange, to establish time of death to clear you. Deacon, call him in. I have to report this as a crime scene now. Weber's going to have a fit if he hears that I'm even here, so I'll have Deacon report that, too."

They made their calls and about a half hour later the place was buzzing with cops, Forensics and the ME team.

"Joe, can you give me a TOD?" Deacon asked formally with Lynn standing behind him.

"Yep, it was in the vicinity of midnight to one a.m., and he was garroted with a thin wire," he said, pointing to the marks around his neck.

Deacon turned to Angelo and me and said, "You two were together at that time?"

"Yep, Angelo was at our home with Penny and me from about 11:30 until he went to bed at two in the morning."

Lynn smiled and said, "That clears the two of you. Oh and Penny, too. I know the three of you had a run in with the victim."

Penny was standing behind me. "Thank you for including me in the murder. I didn't like the man but I wouldn't kill him. Well… maybe." She smiled.

"Careful what you say right now. Even a joke can be taken seriously. I'll need statements from all of you. We need to get this place checked out and the body removed before the press vultures get a whiff of this." She looked at Angelo. "You thought a bad review would hurt your business, just think what murder will do for it."

I've seen Angelo in different moods, but never as sad looking as he was then. I said, "Angelo, we'll work through this. Lynn, Deacon and I will get this solved, and you can get back to business."

The shift leader of the CSI asked us to move out of the crime scene, so we went to the lobby.

"I'm sure he had lots of people who hated him, so there are lots of suspects. We'll need to see what he was doing after he left last night," Deacon said.

Pasta Murders

"I noticed he wrote his thoughts about his visit here in a little book. Maybe he wrote what he was going to do," I offered.

"Good idea, I'll see if they found the book on him," Lynn said and went back into the dining room.

After a couple minutes of standing, Lynn came back out and said, "The book's missing. They didn't find anything on him. Oh, and Joe Lange said that Horn was forced to eat the spaghetti, lots of it. Angelo, I'm sure you don't leave spaghetti lying around."

"No, any left when we close is tossed. It would have had to be prepared or brought in."

"Well, this is taking an interesting twist. He was forced to eat the food, and then the killer came up behind him and strangled him with a wire. But why here, and by whom? Angelo, can you think of any of your staff who might have had reason to lure him here and kill him?"

"Wow, I don't know my staff that well. They've only worked for me a little over a month. I couldn't say if anybody had a motive."

"I'll need to have everyone who worked last night called in for questioning. Can you take care of that Angelo?" Deacon asked.

"Sure can. I'll call now. Most of them will be in soon for opening anyway. I'll call the rest in."

"Angelo, I'm afraid you may not be able to open until we clear the crime scene," Lynn said. "I'll try and clear the parking lot of the Coroner's bus and a few cop cars. CSI will be here until they're finished. If they say it's alright, maybe you can open."

"I think I'll just close for a day or two. I'm not sure how people will react to eating where a man was murdered. I can put up a sign saying we are having a problem with plumbing. That should give people a good enough reason for our being closed."

"It's going to make the news. This man was a big wig in town. People are going to know he died here," I said.

"Yeah, I'll just close up and wait it out." Angelo went to call his employees.

"That man is not happy," Deacon said.

"This was his dream, and he finally got it. Now this jerk comes in and messes up everything for him. I wouldn't be happy either," I said, feeling like crap.

"Okay, we need to interview the employees and see what we can find," Lynn said, breaking the tension.

I turned to Penny. "Well, looks like we found out how we're going to spend our Sunday."

"That's all right. We need to help our friend. I know you'll catch the killer. Murder is your curse." She gave a tiny smile, knowing I hated the curse thing. She always brought up the fact that murder followed me around and never let me forget it. For that matter, neither did anyone else.

An hour later, most of the employees were seated in the dining room which had been cleared by CSI. Two were missing according to Angelo. They weren't scheduled to work today so they were probably off somewhere. Angelo left them a message to call or come in.

Pasta Murders

Deacon called for silence and said, "I'm Detective DeAngelo, and this is Detective Lieutenant Carter." He pointed to Lynn. "I'm sure you know by now that a man was murdered here late last night. I'll need to talk to each of you and get your statements as to where you were. I'll start with you." He pointed to Lonnie, the girl who waited our table last night. "While we're questioning, please keep the talk to yourselves."

Deacon and Lynn took the girl to a side room where it was private and quiet. I followed, and Penny stayed with Angelo in the dining room.

"Hi, Lonnie," Deacon said. "I know you waited on us last night, and you did an excellent job." The girl smiled and waited. "What did you do after Horn and our group left?"

She cleared her throat and said, "I cleaned the tables in my area. Cashed out, and then Angelo said I could leave. I went home and changed clothes then went with a couple friends to a club on Paradise Road. We were there from about eleven until nearly three."

Lynn handed her a note pad and asked her to write down the names of her friends to provide an alibi. Lonnie worked on the names then handed the pad back to Lynn.

"Lonnie, I don't believe you had anything to do with this, but do you know if anyone talked about Horn after he left?"

"Just a few people who had contact with him while he was here. They didn't have many nice things to say about him."

Chapter 6

Lynn allowed Lonnie to leave and called in the next employee, Harvey Rush. He was the manager of the night crew, and his job was to see everything ran smoothly. He had worked the night before as manager until Angelo took over to be sure all went well with Horn.

Harvey sat and didn't smile or make any kind of a face. I thought he would be good in a poker game, no expressions. Lynn sat in front of him and leaned forward.

"Hello, Harvey. How are you doing this morning?" she asked.

"I'm good. Considering the reason I'm here. I was supposed to have the day off."

"Well, we won't keep you any longer than we need to. Now, tell me about last night. Did you have any contact with Alfred Horn?"

He sat straight and formal. "I did not. He was in Cathy's section, and I was relegated to the back of the dining room. As assistant, I took care of half of the dining crew. Mr. DeMarko took the other half, which included Mr. Horn's table. I had no contact with him."

"Did you resent being dropped in authority?" Deacon asked.

"No, we do what we have to. Mr. DeMarko wanted it to be a perfect night for the critic, so I agreed to step down."

Pasta Murders

"Did you know the victim before last night?"

"I've read his column. I thought he was unfair with the establishments he reviewed. I knew the people who worked at some of them. They didn't deserve the bad reviews."

"So you didn't like the man?"

"I was one of many who didn't like him, but I'm not a killer."

"Where were you after the restaurant closed last night?"

"Sorry, I don't have an alibi. I was alone last night. I don't have many friends that I socialize with. I went home and read a book, then to bed around one."

"I guess we can't check that out," Lynn said.

"No, I guess you can't," he replied.

"Where do you live?"

"Up in in North Vegas."

"What route did you take going home and what time?" Deacon asked.

"I drove out Flamingo to the strip and up past Charleston. I got to my home around eleven."

"Okay, you can go, thank you." He left the room. Lynn looked at Deacon and said, "We can check the traffic cameras to see if he passed any of them. Get a make on his car and check it."

Deacon agreed and went out to ask. Lynn left to call another employee.

We spent about an hour talking to the employees but didn't learn anything that would give us a lead to go on. Everyone had about the same statements, either they didn't like him or they didn't have contact with him.

Deacon reported that he had called in to find out where Horn lived. He was a resident of one of the new and expensive tower condos that were starting to pop up around Vegas. "That place has tight security and surveillance, so it'll be easy to see what Horn's activities were last night."

"Good, because I don't think there's much here to go on. Hopefully CSI will come up with something from the crime scene. I guess we can go to his apartment now." Lynn stood, shakily, trying to balance her pregnancy bump.

"Hon, you really should take it easy," Deacon said with concern.

"I'm not going to push myself. I'll be careful," she replied.

I pulled her chair back so she could get by. She smiled and thanked me. "So, Jim did any of these people ring your chime?"

"Not really. They all either disliked the man or didn't care one way or the other. Everyone except Harvey Rush had a good alibi. It's hard to live in Las Vegas without being around someone. He's a loner, reads books instead of partying. Didn't like Horn's treatment of other restaurant employees he knows. He's the only one who stood out for me, but it's all conjecture for now."

"Yeah, that's my take, too. So shall we go check out Horn's fancy living quarters?" she asked.

I went out to Penny and Angelo sitting alone in the corner of the dining room, both looking unhappy.

Pasta Murders

"Angelo, we have no problem with your employees, but we need to check on a few things before we make a determination. We're going to Horn's place to see if there's anything that could help there. Penny, if you could take the van home, I'll catch a ride with Lynn and Deacon."

"I can handle that," she replied.

"Angelo, rather than staying by yourself until this is over, would you like to stay in the guesthouse again? Just for a few days," I said, hoping he wouldn't brood about the incident by himself.

"That would be real nice, Mr. R. I'll think about it but I may want to be alone," he said.

"Well, think about it. The door's always open for you. Besides, Willy likes your company."

Angelo got a big smile at that and said, "Yeah, he's good company. Maybe I'll get a dog, too."

Penny laughed. "You do, and Willy will be jealous. Having a dog is relaxing to your soul, but it's also a lot of work."

Lynn came over. "Angelo, we're finished with your people. You can keep them here or let them go home. Up to you."

"Thanks, I may just give them the time off. I know it hurts their pay, but I can't open now after all this."

"Give them time off with pay, take it out of business expenses. Keep your employees happy," I said.

"Yeah, this isn't their fault. Damn Horn. I wish I never heard of him," Angelo said, then stood. "I'll go

42

turn my people loose and make a sign for the front door saying we'll be closed for a couple days."

He went off looking even sadder than before. I was getting madder about the whole situation and wanting a piece of the killer myself. I just hoped Angelo didn't decide to bring in family connections right now. Lynn wouldn't like that. She had a past history with her father and the mob he worked for. I had used Angelo's connections many times in the past, but I might need them soon to get this resolved.

Penny stood also and kissed my cheek. "Get the killer for Angelo. Make him a happy man again," she said.

"I'll do that. I don't like seeing him this way. Be careful driving home. I'll be there when I can."

I kissed her back, and she said good-bye to Lynn and Deacon then went out of the building.

"Shall we go?" I asked.

Lynn yelled to Angelo, "We're leaving. Talk later."

He was with his people and waved to us. The employees didn't look happy, but getting a day or two off with pay would help.

We went to Deacon's big pick-up truck. I said, "Couldn't bring the Prius?"

"I was in a rush to get here. People move faster with a truck barreling down behind them with flashers and sirens," he said with a grin. We got in, I sat in the small rear seating which I hated, being a little claustrophobic and overweight for the cramped quarters.

Pasta Murders

We drove out Flamingo and up the strip to the new high rise apartments that were constructed last year. It was an expensive building to live in, but it was occupied by rich people who could afford it.

"Interesting that Horn lived here. I'm sure his salary at the newspaper isn't so much that he could afford this place. Maybe he has something going on that he doesn't tell people about."

"*Had* something and *didn't* tell, Jim. He's dead and in the past tense now. For a writer, you should know all this stuff," Lynn said with a smirk.

"Thank you for correcting me. I'll be more careful in the future."

We arrived at the entrance to the huge buildings. Three towers, all overlooking the strip. A perfect view of Sin City from any direction. A valet came out, but Deacon waved him off and put the "Police Business" sign in his window. We went into the lobby. It was all shiny and full of glass and chrome. Deacon asked the man at the counter to see the head of security. He flashed his badge to make it official.

After a few minutes a tall man in a black suit came out of a door and up to Deacon.

"Officer, how may I help you?" he asked curtly.

"It's *Detective* DeAngelo, and this is Lieutenant Carter, homicide, and this man is a civilian consultant."

"Homicide? I've had no reports of any crimes in the building." He blinked nervously at the thought.

"No, not in your building, outside of. Alfred Horn was murdered early this morning, and we understand he lived here." Lynn spoke this time.

"Alfred! He was murdered, how?"

"We're still investigating. Right now we need to see if you have any record or video of Mr. Horn's activities last night from about eleven until two in the morning."

"Yes, of course." He went to the front desk and pulled the book from the attendant. "We have strict policies about logging our residents and their guests in, coming and going. The residents have all agreed for their safety to abide by these policies."

He scanned the books and finally stopped. "Yes, here it is. Mr. Horn arrived at eleven-fifteen and was in his apartment until he went out at midnight. He never returned, but of course we know why."

"Was he alone both times?" I asked.

"According to the book he was. But there is one entry of a person inquiring about Mr. Horn at eleven-thirty. He was told Mr. Horn was in, and he left."

*

Chapter 7

"Do you have the video from that time?" Deacon asked.

"Of course, we keep two weeks' worth of surveillance before we recycle the tapes. I presume you want to see this man?"

"That would be the plan. May we?" Deacon asked. "I'm sorry, I didn't get your name."

"I didn't give it, but I'm Daniel Keller. Head of security."

45

Pasta Murders

"Thank you, Mr. Keller. Shall we see the videos now?"

"Since it was Mr. Horn who's now deceased, I won't bother to ask for a warrant. Follow me please." He turned back to the door he came out of, and we followed. The door led to a long hallway with glass on both sides providing views of offices with people at their desks, working.

"Lots of activity for a high rise condo?" Lynn asked.

"This is all part of the corporation that owns the building. They occupy the entire first floor and a couple penthouse apartments for clients. They have money and like to show it off." He said that with a hint of distaste.

He came to a door at the end of the hall and keyed in his card. We heard a very loud click of the locks, and he opened the door. We entered the room that looked like something out of a super spy movie. There were high definition TV monitors all over the walls, each, I presumed, from cameras in the towers on the floors. There were about five people either manning the consoles for the monitors or just working at their keyboards.

"We know what goes on in every floor of the building. By switching around we can see in the stairwells or at the outside doors to shipping and entrances. The first three floors are commercial offices and businesses. Then we have the shopping promenade in this tower, and it's usually busy. Above that are the apartments. The entrance you came through is for the apartments only. The public can get to the shopping area and offices through a different entrance."

He flipped switches and tapped the keyboards as the biggest monitor came to life with an image of the main lobby. We watched as a man came to the desk, Horn. "This is when Horn entered at eleven." He fast forwarded it to another man entering. "This is the mystery man."

"Can you change angles so we can see his face?" Deacon asked.

"Of course," he said with a little huffiness.

He tapped at the keyboard, and the video switched to behind the desk clerk, showing the visitor. He had a baseball cap pulled low, a beard and sunglasses.

"Who the hell wears sunglasses at night" Lynn asked.

"Celebrities," I responded. She gave me a dirty look. I just smiled.

"Well, he's not a celebrity. He's hiding his face. He knows he'll be on camera. Mr. Keller, can you do a printout on him?"

"Certainly." He did more key tapping. A printer started up and spit out a print. He picked it up and handed it to Deacon.

"Can you print one of his back so we can examine his features?"

Keller obliged and gave her the print. Lynn studied it, then said, "Well, we can see his shoes or I should say boots. It may help later. Thank you, Mr. Keller. I may have our forensic people come by to get a copy of that section of video, if that's all right with you."

"Hold on," he said then did some more magic on the keyboard. After a few moments he pulled a CD disc out of a slot in one of the computers. "Here's the copy to save your people time."

"Well, I'm impressed. Thank you again. Now, may we see his apartment?"

He paused for a moment. "I suppose you'll come barreling in here with a whole team of CSI to tear into his expensive apartment. I will let you in if you promise to be gentle with it. The company will have to sell it again. Selling an apartment of a murdered man is bad enough, but one that was torn apart by your people will be a most difficult sale."

"I promise you'll never know we were in there. Of course, you'll have to find his family to have the furnishings removed."

He gave a pained look. "More people tramping around. Oh, well. Come, I'll let you in." He went past us, out of the room and then to the elevators that went up to the apartments.

We got in, and he pushed the button for the tenth floor. The elevator quickly ascended. It took no time at all, and my stomach was left somewhere around the fifth floor. We got off the elevator, and Keller led us to a door near the elevators. He pulled another card from his pocket and pushed it in the door lock release.

"Does your card open all the doors of this place?" Lynn asked.

Bob Moats

"As head of security, I do have access to all the apartments in the three towers. I never use it unless a resident locks himself or herself out of their apartment. I don't advertise that this card opens all doors. The residents might have a problem with that. Most of them are filthy rich and have many expensive objects of art and collections."

"But they'd have to trust you, right?" Deacon asked.

"Yes, with my position here, I have to be the utmost honest person around. Totally trustworthy."

"A real boy scout you are," Lynn quipped.

We entered the apartment and stood just in the door staring at all the mess of the room. It looked like the place was ransacked.

"What the hell!" Keller exploded. "How could this happen"

"I think you should go down and check your surveillance tapes for this floor. Just to see who may have been up here," I said.

He rushed out of the room and was gone. "Nervous man, I'd say." I said.

We walked around the mess on the floor and looked into the other rooms, each of us taking an area of the apartment.

"I'll have CSI in here shortly. I just called. Don't make a mess before they get here." Lynn laughed aloud and then went to the kitchen.

Deacon came over to me. "I can't figure what someone would want with all this junk. Horn must have collected this stuff for years. Looks like he was a hoarder, judging by some of this crap. This doesn't figure into his death at the restaurant, why someone would break in and tear the place apart after killing him."

"Maybe they tortured him to find whatever they wanted in this mess. He wouldn't talk so they killed him and came here to tear into the place," I replied.

I studied the mess. There were knick-knacks that my Grandmother would have put on her shelves, gathering dust. I knew that most of the statues scattered around the room weren't of any value. They looked like they were bought at yard sales. There were books, ones I had read years before. They weren't of any value, unless they had money stashed between the pages. Then there were the African art objects. I recognized the fertility God statues. I wasn't touching those. I rummaged around the room finding lots of photos, mostly four by six size, of Horn and another man. They looked very cozy together. Could Horn have been gay?

Lynn came back into the room. "Okay, let's vacate the apartment for CSI to examine. We can go check with Keller to see if he got a visual on this floor." She went to the door and out to the hall. We followed her to the elevator and down to the main floor. I picked up my stomach at the fifth floor.

Keller let us into the security office. He was running the videos of the evening from midnight when Horn left to this morning. He wasn't happy that someone got past their security to commit a crime. He had to head this off before his bosses or the residents found out.

"My job is toast if someone got in without us knowing," he said. "I've assembled the best in security people and equipment, and then this happens."

Keller ran the tapes forward until he found a blip around three in the morning. It was a cleaning person, a man pushing a cart who stopped at Horn's apartment. He put a card in the door and opened it, went in and was in the room for about an hour, according to the tape. He came out and moved away. Keller did his best to follow the man, but he went out a door to the stairwell as Keller switched views. The video went blank.

"What the hell?" he said. He turned to one of the men in the room and said to go check the stairwell on that floor. The man got up and went out. Keller switched to that floor, and it was still blank. "The man must have covered the cameras. Damn. This is not good."

We watched as the blank screen changed to an image of the security man pulling the cover from the camera. "Yep, he covered the thing with a paper. Not very clever," Keller said.

"Clever enough to block your sight," I said.

He looked at me and frowned. "Yes, it worked didn't it?"

Lynn's cellphone buzzed. She answered, listened and hung up. "CSI is here and they need to get in. I'll have them dust the camera that was covered. I don't think there will be any prints, but you never know. Can you let them in?"

"Sure," Keller said, then looked back to the video screen. "This is not good. Not good at all."

*

Chapter 8

Lynn and Deacon went up with the CSI team to examine the apartment. I waited downstairs in the lobby, watching the rich and famous entering and leaving the place. I recognized a few people, some I didn't. I went outside the building and watched the valets parking the cars of the rich and famous. It's fun to have someone park your car for you, then bring it back in one piece. I know, I've used valet a number of times around Vegas.

I wondered how the mystery man got into the building in order to masquerade as a cleaning person. Then he had to know which cameras to cover and be able to get into Horn's apartment. This person must have known Horn's schedule and habits. This was no simple robbery or murder, this had timing and motive. Horn was bound, stuffed with pasta, then murdered.

The killer came to Horn's apartment to find something, but why take Horn to Angelo's restaurant? The killer could have murdered Horn in his own apartment and then searched the place. This was not making sense. Could there be two crimes here? One the murder, one the ransacking of the apartment. By whom and why?

Horn needed to be investigated further. And who was the other man in the photos? A lover of Horn's? Was Horn gay? I could ask around the Review-Journal of his co-workers to see. If they even knew. Horn seemed like a very private person. Would anyone really know him?

I was surprised to see a familiar man entering the building. It was the other man in Horn's photos. I moved quickly and followed him to the elevators after he waved to the man at the desk. He must be a resident or well known by the desk clerks. I followed him into the elevator and saw he pressed floor ten. He looked at me and smiled.

"You need a floor?" he asked politely.

"Ten is fine, thank you," I replied. I left my stomach on five again.

The doors opened, and I could see a bit of commotion in the hallway outside of Horn's apartment. Lynn and Deacon were talking to a couple men from the CSI team. I lingered behind the man as he stepped out of the elevator. When he saw the people standing there with uniforms on, he started to turn back to the elevator. I stood in front of him.

"I don't think you should leave," I said.

He started to push me. Deacon saw this and rushed over, grabbing the man before he could get back on the elevator

"Let me go!" the man exclaimed, trying to free himself from Deacon's grasp.

"Calm down," Deacon yelled as the man struggled.

Lynn came over. "What's going on?"

Pasta Murders

"This man is in a number of photos in Horn's apartment, looking cozy with Horn," I said.

That seemed to calm the man. He ceased his struggles and said, "I'm a friend of Alfred's, that's all. What is this about? And who are you people?"

"We're the police. How well did you know Horn?" Deacon asked.

"As I said, I'm a friend. I was coming to see him. We're supposed to go out for lunch."

Deacon released the man. He straightened his clothing and stood calmly.

"Your name, please?" Lynn asked.

"Taylor Higgs. You are?"

"Lieutenant Carter, homicide."

The man went pale and looked shocked. "Oh my God, is Alfred all right? Why are you here?"

"Mr. Higgs, I regret to inform you that Mr. Horn was murdered last night."

The man stood for a moment with his mouth open, then he started to have a panic attack.

"No! It can't be, not Alfred. Tell me he's all right! Tell me this is some joke that Alfred set up! NO!!"

He dropped to the floor, crying aloud. We watched him with sympathy. He evidently knew Horn better than he let on. Deacon pulled him up, took him to the apartment and sat him on a chair by the door. He was still sobbing and weaving back and forth. I had seen lots of people being told their loved ones or friends were killed, but he seemed to take it very hard.

He asked between chokes of air, "What happened? I have to know?"

"We're investigating, if you could maybe help us find his killer, it would help. We'll need to take you to our precinct to question you," Lynn said.

The man looked around to the room and went silent. "Was this how you found the room?" he finally asked.

"Yes, the apartment was trashed. It's how we found it."

"The bastards, they did this," he said.

"Who?" Lynn asked.

"The Neo-Nazis. They've been on Alfred's case since they found out he was gay. I don't know how, but they did." He started rocking and crying again.

Lynn called for a uniform to take Higgs to the precinct and watch him closely in case he did something stupid, like try to kill himself. The cop nodded and helped Higgs up and out.

"Nazi skin heads? Would they go to all the trouble to lure Horn into Momma Mia, kill him, then trash his apartment? They may need to be questioned, but I don't think they would have set this up," Deacon said.

"Well, we have to find out who they are. I personally don't know of any Neo-Nazis in Vegas. Not even in past cases," Lynn said. "But that doesn't mean they aren't out there."

"I'll call the gang squad. They may know. If not, we could just advertise for applicants," Deacon said with a grin.

Pasta Murders

Lynn gave him the evil-eye and walked away. She went back in the apartment and told the CSI supervisor that we were leaving and to contact Keller in security when they were finished. He agreed, and we went to the elevator.

Back on the street level we got into Deacon's truck. "Shall we go talk to Horn's boyfriend or get lunch?" he asked.

"Drive through Hot-N-Now and grab some burgers. We don't want to leave Mr. Higgs stewing all afternoon. Bad enough he lost a loved one," Lynn said.

Deacon pulled out of the huge circular drive and onto Las Vegas Boulevard. He went straight to the nearest Hot-N-Now on Maryland and turned into the drive through. He ordered all of us burgers and fries and paid. A first for Deacon.

"You can eat now as we drive or wait till we get to the precinct," Lynn said as she handed my food to me.

"Did you get a burger for Higgs? He had plans to go to lunch with the late Mr. Horn, and now he sits in a police station," I said, looking at my food.

Deacon said, "I can give him one of my burgers. I ordered three."

"Are you sure you won't starve?" I asked.

Lynn said, "I'll give him my fries. They won't settle well anyway. The baby is being picky about what I eat."

"Good, now Mr. Higgs should at least be happy for the offer. Hopefully," I said.

A few minutes later Deacon pulled into the police precinct and parked. We went in the back door, past the same desk sergeant who must live there. He nodded at us and smiled at me. That worried me.

We went into the homicide squad room and to Lynn's office. She saw Captain Weber coming down the hall and said, "Uh oh." She went to the desk in the squad room Weber assigned to her until she had the baby and sat. Deacon grinned and went into Lynn's office.

"Nice, you don't get a promotion, but at least an office," I said.

"Yeah, with Lynn siting out there glaring at me. I'd close the curtains but that would piss her off. You don't want to piss off a pregnant woman, especially Lynn."

Weber came through the door into the squad room and yelled for Lynn to join him in her office. She stood and followed him.

"Richards, are you helping with the Horn case?" he said with his usual bellow.

"How did you know about the Horn case?" I asked.

"Charlie Ramsey at the Review-Journal is a friend. He called me about it. I checked with some of the uniforms that were at Angelo's restaurant and got the details. Now, Lynn, fill me in." He sat in the chair in front of her desk. Deacon was sitting in Lynn's chair behind the desk, but got up quickly and let her sit.

Pasta Murders

"Captain, I was just observing," she said. "Deacon is primary on the case. Jim woke us this morning, saying that Angelo called him. I went to the restaurant with Deacon, but not to work."

Weber sat a moment, then smiled. "Don't try to fool me, Lynn. I'm sure you stuck your nose in and helped. I gave you a desk job for your own health, but I can't stop you from what you're good at."

I could almost see Lynn breathe easier hearing Weber say that. "Yes, sir. Angelo is a friend, and we want to clear his name and his restaurant."

"I've eaten there, and the food is fantastic. Hate to see the place get a black eye. So tell me everything you've learned so far."

Lynn related the entire episode up to coming into the precinct. She did, however, leave out the burgers. Weber eyed the bags and smiled.

"We knew that Higgs was supposed to go to lunch with Horn and hated to see him starve if he's going to help us. So we stopped and got him some food," Lynn said sheepishly.

"Well, enjoy your lunch and fill me in on your questioning of Higgs. I have work to do." He stood and quickly disappeared out of the office. That man never stayed in one place for very long.

*

Chapter 9

Lynn sat back and took a deep breath. "I never know with that man. He's kind hearted, but has a screw loose sometimes."

I liked Weber. He actually was a kind person. He was the arch nemesis of Trapper from when Trapper was a young cop here in Vegas years ago. Trapper was a wild child and would bring hookers into the holding area for…well, that was history, and legends grew from that time. Weber found out, but too late when Trapper had already left Vegas to go to Michigan.

"Now we need to talk to Higgs," Deacon said. "Oh, am I still primary on this case or has Weber given you permission to take over?"

"Bunny bear, I'll let you take credit for this case. But I get to unofficially lead it."

"I'll ignore the bunny bear comment and accept your kind offer," he said.

We went out to find where they had put Higgs. One of the uniforms that had been at the condos said he was in interrogation 3. We went there, and Lynn let me come in with them. I sat by the door.

Lynn and Deacon sat at the table across from Higgs, and Lynn put the burger bag in front of him. He stared at it, and Lynn said, "Go ahead and eat. You'll be here for a while."

Higgs grabbed the bag and pulled out the burger and fries, spreading them on the table. He was wolfing down the food as he asked, "What can I do to help find the bastard who killed Alfred?" He wiped his mouth with the napkin and swallowed.

"Okay, let's start with who you think may have killed him?" Lynn asked.

"As I said, it could be the Neo-Nazis. They had been harassing him for the last week. Somehow they found out he was gay and just didn't like him."

"How were they harassing him?"

"Letters, emails, phone calls late at night. No actual contact with him, the spineless bastards." He took another bite of the burger and stuffed four French fries into his mouth.

Lynn smiled as she watched the man eat like it was his last meal. "What was the gist of the threats? Any life threatening comments?"

Higgs paused, thinking. "Well, no, they didn't say they would kill him outright. But they said horrible things about his lifestyle and how he should get out of Vegas. Now that's funny. Sin City, full of sinners and a good number of gays and transvestites, and they think he's a bad example. Dumb shits." He stuffed a bunch of fries in his mouth and washed them down with the cup of water Deacon had given him.

"Thank you for the food. It's good of you," he said.

Lynn looked at me and smiled. "No problem. Now suppose that Higgs wasn't killed by the Nazis. Who else may have wanted him dead?"

"Oh, God, who didn't want him dead? He was a restaurant critic, and he would tear into most of the restaurants in town. If they didn't have clean restrooms, he'd make a big deal out of it. He would complain about poor help or wait staff that was too slow for his liking. I talked to him last night right after he left the restaurant he was visiting."

We all perked up on that. We waited for him to take a big bite of burger, chew, swallow and continue.

"What did he say?" I asked impatiently.

"Huh? Oh, he liked his visit. He was trying to be hard on everyone. That was his way, be a bastard and see if he got good treatment in return. He did, no matter how hard he goaded the owner and the wait staff. They all were polite and efficient through his entire visit. He could be really hard on people, which is why he wasn't well-liked."

"So he would have given Momma Mia a good review?" I asked.

"Oh, sure, he did. He wrote it all down in his Moleskin book. He kept all his notes in that book. You did find his book, didn't you?"

Lynn said, "We found nothing on him. Would he have left the book anywhere else?"

"Nope, he carried it everywhere he went. It was his diary, or journal, and he had it filled with all sorts of things."

Lynn looked at Deacon. "We need to find that book. Talk to CSI again, see if they found it."

Deacon said he would.

I was happy that Horn gave Angelo's restaurant a good review, or would have if he'd lived. I'd tell Angelo about it later.

Pasta Murders

"Okay, suppose the Nazis didn't trash Horn's apartment. What would someone else want from that place? What was important enough to kill him for?"

Higgs swallowed the last of the burgers and fries, crumpled the papers and bag and looked for a place to dispose of it. Deacon took the bag from him and tossed it in the receptacle in the room.

"Important enough to actually kill him? I have no idea. Other than the fact that he wasn't liked for what he did, he had nothing that I know of that would be the cause of his death. No money, no gold or jewelry worth killing for."

"Higgs, we need help here. You were close to Horn. Can't you think of anything that might have caused someone to murder him and trash his place?"

Higgs went silent and stared at the table in front of him. A good sign that he knew more than he was telling.

"I hate to say it, Taylor, but you are our number one suspect right now," Lynn said. I figured she was hoping to stir Higgs up.

His head snapped up, and he got loud. "I would never, ever hurt Alfred. He was the love of my life, and I didn't kill him. I want to know who did just as much as you. But I don't know." He went silent again, but stared at Lynn this time.

"What line of work are you in?" Lynn asked.

"I work for the Las Vegas Sun newspaper. I'm an entertainment columnist. I report on bands and events going on in Vegas."

"A competitive newspaper. And you were lovers. How did Horn take to the fact that you worked for the Sun?"

"Oh, come on. That's not even a good question! We were journalists, that's all. I could have worked for the New York Times for all Alfred cared. Don't try and pin this on me. I loved the man and would never harm him."

"Okay, Mr. Higgs, we appreciate your cooperation. We're sorry for your loss, and if you remember anything or find out anything that may help to catch his killer, let us know. I'll have an officer take you back to your car at the condos." Lynn stood, followed by Deacon and me. We went out, and Lynn called a uniform over and told him to take the man to where ever he wanted to go.

We stood watching Higgs leave with the officer. "I don't think he had anything to do with Horn's murder, but I think he knows something," Lynn said. "I don't know why he won't tell. We need to watch him."

She called to Detective Greg Warren and filled him in on the case. She wanted him to watch Higgs and report anything he might find out.

"I'll get on it. I've read Higgs' column. He's good," Warren said then went out of the squad room.

"So, it appears that Horn would have given Angelo a good review. Too bad he didn't live long enough to write it," Deacon said.

"Maybe it's in his notebook. The paper could print it as his last review," I said.

Pasta Murders

"I don't know, that sounds a bit morbid to me. A review by a dead man? Even if it is favorable for Angelo, after the murder in his restaurant and a dead man's review, it's not looking good for the restaurant," Lynn said with a smile.

"Okay, point taken. I just want to see Momma Mia come out of this without a smear," I replied.

"So are the burgers we bought for ourselves still in the office?" Lynn asked.

Deacon went in and came out with the extra bags he'd hidden when Weber came by. "Shall we go to the lunch room and reheat them?"

"'Reheated French fries? That's not something I want to eat, but I'm hungry. So let's go nuke the puppies," I said.

We went to the lunch room that was also part of a store room. It had two drink machines, one coffee machine and one snack machine. It was the best that LVMPD could provide for this precinct. There were other precincts in town, some more important than others. This one was an older building and had fewer men than the headquarters uptown. We reheated our food and sat by the window trying to eat the soggy fries and flat burgers.

"This is Weber's fault. We could have had a nice lunch if he hadn't shown up," Deacon said.

"Just enjoy the food," Lynn said. "It's better than the crap from the machines."

"True. So Horn was killed in Momma Mia, and his apartment was trashed. Someone wanted something that Horn wasn't willing to give up," Deacon said.

"Or he did give it up, and they still had to find the mysterious booty. I'm betting on blackmail photos," I said as I tried to down the limp French fries.

"Now, that's the best I have heard so far. Horn was blackmailing someone in the restaurant industry. Maybe for money to live as lavishly as he was. I should have asked Higgs about Horn's finances and his lifestyle. I'll have Warren run a check on Horn's finances. And maybe Higgs, also."

Lynn's cell phone buzzed. She answered, listened, and hung up. "Damn, that was Warren. Higgs tried to run his car into a pole. He's in the hospital, and he's critical."

*

Chapter 10

"If Higgs really wanted to kill himself, he could have jumped off the Stratosphere Tower. Why run into a power pole and run the risk of just injuring himself?" Lynn said as we stood in the hallway of LV Medical where we met Greg Warren who filled us in.

"Who knows if he was even trying to take his own life?" I offered.

"Well, I have CSI going over the car and examining the video from the traffic cameras. He's in a coma, so we won't get much from him," she said then went silent.

We waited until a doctor emerged from the operating room. He saw Lynn and came to us.

Pasta Murders

"Lynn, how are you today?" he asked, looking at Lynn's baby bump.

She smiled. "Feeling so-so. How is Higgs? Is he going to make it?"

"He's in a coma for now. Only time will tell. Sorry I don't have anything better to tell you. He took a bad blow to the head despite the air bag. The pole came down, caved the roof of his car and nearly crushed his skull. Honestly, if he comes out of the coma, he still may not be able to talk or comprehend anything. Too early to form a prognosis."

"Thanks, Doc. Let me know if there's any change."

"I will," he said and walked off.

"Did Higgs do this deliberately? And for what reason? Did he know something that he just couldn't bear to live with?" Lynn sat down on a bench in the hallway.

"You ask a lot of questions," I said with a smile. "We'll never know the answers if he dies."

"Thanks Jim, you're always a ray of sunshine," she said with a smirk. She looked at Greg Warren and asked, "Did you follow him from the precinct or from the condos?"

"I caught up with him at his car and followed him from there. He was fine, then all of a sudden he started driving erratically and sped up. He ran straight into the pole over on Sahara."

"Sahara? Did he live in that area?" Deacon asked.

"No, while I was waiting for you to get here I made a check of his wallet. He lived in the same condo building as Horn."

"So why was he on Sahara? Was he going to meet someone or…? Crap, I don't know. Let's wait until CSI finds something with the car or surveillance video," Lynn said, looking miserable.

"Baby acting up?" Deacon asked as he sat next to her.

"A little, I'll be all right," she replied.

"It's getting late. Why don't you go home and rest? I'll take care of this mess."

"Yeah, that sounds like a good idea. You'll be able to watch Higgs and check with CSI. I'll have a patrol car take me home. You take the unmarked car."

Deacon helped her stand up and called for a car to come get her. They went to the emergency lobby front door and waited for the patrol car to arrive. Deacon put Lynn in and they drove off. He came back to Gregg and me still standing in the waiting room.

"I wish she'd take a maternity leave. She's not doing well. I hope she's all right," Deacon said with a long face. "She's tough, but I think she's putting up a front for me and the rest of the squad."

"Deacon, you have the best doctors watching over her. I'm sure they'd know if something was wrong," I said hoping, to soothe him.

"Yeah, she's due for another check-up day after tomorrow. We'll see how that goes."

Pasta Murders

"Do you want me to call CSI and see if we can get some word on this?" Warren asked.

"Sure, Gregg, that would be good."

Warren went out of the ER and made a call. We watched all the people in the waiting room, hoping to get in for whatever ailment they had. I could tell a few must be drug addicts by the way they were suffering, probably from withdrawals. I felt sorry for those who allowed themselves to get hooked on drugs. It was stupid and expensive. If the government would spend some money on stopping drug trafficking instead of fighting all these needless wars, there might be a good number of people saved. Both from war and from drugs. But I never figured politicians had any brains, so the stupidity goes on.

Warren came back after a few minutes and said, "Got something interesting." He paused for effect.

"What, Greg? I'm not in the mood for guessing games," Deacon growled.

"CSI found tampering on Higgs' brakes and steering. Looks like we have an attempted homicide," he said with a grin.

"Well, isn't this a hoot?" Deacon said.

"A hoot?" I asked, "Are you still in the 19th century?"

"You know what I mean," he said with a glare at me. "Higgs must have had something to do with Horn's death, or know something about it. Otherwise why would someone want to kill him, too? And why this way? A gunshot to the head would be quicker."

"Maybe they wanted it to be more dramatic," I said, waiting for Deacon to think through all the implications.

"Drama is not what we need right now. We need to figure out what Horn had that others wanted. We need to dig into Horn's past and see what we can come up with. Higgs isn't going anywhere, so we don't have to wait here. Let's go to the Review-Journal and talk to Horn's editor. Greg, go see what CSI came up with on the car." Greg agreed and left. "Shall we go play news men?"

"It will be a hoot," I replied with a smile.

"I'm sorry it even came out. You'll be saying that all day, won't you?"

"Hoot mon!" I said in my best Scottish brogue, and was ready for him to swing at me. He did, and I ducked.

"Are you coming?" he asked and went out of the waiting room. I followed.

We drove over to the offices of the Las Vegas Review-Journal, one of the oldest newspapers in Vegas. I read it every morning when I could just to see what crimes were going on in town. I also read the entertainment columns to see who was making a fuss in the city. Celebrities loved to come to town and get into some kind of trouble just for the publicity.

We went in the building and over to the reception desk. Deacon flashed his badge and asked, "May we see the editor for the food section of the paper?"

"Is this about Mr. Horn?" the attractive girl behind the counter asked.

Pasta Murders

"Yes, it is."

"I'll call Mr. Morgan. He was Mr. Horn's boss." She got on the phone and called.

About five minutes later a short, plain looking woman came to us and said, "Mr. Morgan will see you. Follow me, please."

We followed her into the inner sanctum of news reporting, down long halls and around people scurrying everywhere. It was Sunday, but the news never rests. We arrived on the fourth level at a glass door with the lettering of the Food and Lifestyle Section offices. We went through and on to another door, this one wood and marked, Jay Morgan, Editor. The plain girl went through the door to an inner vestibule and then to her desk. She buzzed on an intercom and announced us.

A nice walnut door opened, and out came a short man with a belly that made mine look thin.

"Welcome officers, come in."

Deacon corrected him, "It's *Detective* and this man is a consultant to the LVMPD. I'm Detective DeAngelo, and this man is Jim Richards. We'd like to talk to you about Alfred Horn."

"I figured as much. Sit, please, grab a chair and sit. We don't stand on formality here. Sit." He went behind an antique desk that looked like it might have been in the newspaper business a long time and sat.

"Jim Richards, the P.I. who saves Vegas from dirty bombs and viruses?"

I said I was.

"Pleasure to meet you. Now ask your questions. I'm willing to help in any way I can. Horn was a valuable member of the team. His columns were the big feature of our Sunday section. In fact, he emailed his column for today's paper last night, I presume just before he died. Terrible shame."

I was surprised by the statement that Horn had sent his column in. I knew most reporters wrote where ever they could and emailed the article in to their editors, but I didn't figure Horn had the time to write his column about Angelo's restaurant and send it so quickly.

"Mr. Morgan, do you have a copy of that column?" I asked.

"Of course." He stood and went to a stack of papers, pulling one and handing it to me.

"Thank you," I said as I found the Food and Lifestyle section. Horn had his column on the front page as always, and I scanned it quickly to see what he thought. At the bottom of the column he always had a system of star ratings for different things, like food, service, ambience and such. I saw it was all good stars, mostly five stars for each listing. Angelo was going to be real happy about this.

"Now what do you need to know?" Morgan asked.

"Well, we have a mystery. Someone killed Horn last night late then trashed his apartment. Would you know why someone would trash his apartment?"

"Looking for something, I presume," he replied.

"That much we figured, but would you know what might be something worth killing him for?"

Morgan sat back and thought for a minute before he answered. "Horn was a man of many faces. He

71

wasn't always a food critic for the newspaper. Years ago he had jobs in many important places, mostly overseas and for the government as a writer. He had access to many government files, a lot of secret stuff. Maybe he had something secret that somebody wanted back."

*

Chapter 11

"Our government? In what capacity?" Deacon asked.

"He wrote reports about various things. Nuclear testing, the cold war with Russia, Presidential speeches, you name it. He was good with his writing, and the government took advantage. Overseas, he was a war correspondent during World War Two. Wrote propaganda for the home team. He also had access to the Congressional Archives for his research. I think he may have found more than he bargained for. He got fed up and quit that field, but he always had a taste for food, so he started in the Washington D.C. area papers bashing local restaurants. He survived a couple years and moved slowly across country to land in Vegas. I knew he was free lancing and grabbed him up for the R-J. He's been here five years now. Sad to see it end."

"How did you find out all this info?" Deacon asked.

Morgan laughed. "Horn was a lush. He drank to excess. And when he was sloshed, he talked too much. He would come in here late nights with his articles, and we'd imbibe in a number of shots of good old Jim Beam. Before the end of the evening, he'd be telling me about his adventures. I should write them all down for a retrospective of his life."

"Lately has he said anything about being worried that he was in trouble or danger?"

"Nope, he didn't come around much after he finally got the hang of email. He was slow starting with it. He was an old fashioned writer, using that old Remington typewriter he carried all through his career. He was a fast typist, and could knock out a column in no time."

"That's probably how he wrote today's column in the less than forty-five minutes that he was in his apartment last night," I said.

"Hell, he could turn one out in twenty minutes. He wrote the whole thing in his head and then just had to type it out. He probably had it written before he even left the restaurant."

Thankfully for Angelo, I thought. And thankfully they published it.

"Could he have had anything top secret that someone wanted?" I asked.

"Could be. He knew a lot of stuff. I'd hate to think our government could have done this. I think it might have been some foreign agency, but that's just my opinion. Now, his contacts with the government ended years ago. What could he have from back then that somebody wanted today?"

Pasta Murders

"Good question," Deacon said. "Thank you for your time on this beautiful Sunday. Are you here all week?"

"I live at this desk. I used to cover the hard core news, crime beat and such, but I'm not as fast as I was. I'm divorced four times, married to the job more than the wives. I'm single and happy now. My job doesn't complain or want expensive gifts. So I'm happy to spend time here." He smiled as his assistant came in interrupting him. She said he had another visitor and then went out.

Deacon and I stood. It was time to leave. Morgan rose and came around his desk to shake our hands. "I'll call if I find out anything," he said as Deacon handed him his card.

We went out of the building and back to the car. "I've had enough for today," Deacon said. "I'm going to check with Warren and then go home to my grumpy big baby. I'll drive you home after I get the truck."

We drove back to the precinct where Deacon dropped off the unmarked car and we got in Deacon's souped-up truck.

"You really enjoy this thing?" I asked.

"Yeah, but it uses too much gas. I may sell it and get a nice family car," he said with a laugh.

"Yep, you have to play the part now, Mr. Dad."

I didn't look but I could tell he was grinning widely. He drove me home, and I got out. "See you in the morning after I go to the office to check the place. Lacey is supposed to be back from vacation tomorrow, and I want to be there to aggravate her.

See ya." I closed the truck door and went to the house.

I entered, and Willy bounced around my feet. I scooped him up and went into the kitchen expecting to find Penny. She wasn't there. I noticed the patio door was open, meaning she was back by our pool.

I went out and stopped by the ugly Greek statue still pouring water into the Koi pond. I grabbed a handful of feed from the can and tossed it into the pond. The jumbo sized gold fish gobbled it up. I didn't hear any splashing in the pool. I went around to find Penny taking a spin around her stripper pole in her favorite bikini.

It was embedded beside the pool by the former owner, a strip burlesque show producer, who threw throw lavish parties there years ago. Penny learned to use the pole back in Michigan when she had a stripper—pardon me—exotic dancer on her local show, and the woman taught her a few maneuvers on it. She managed to get the pole that was used on that show installed in our family room, and she would entertain me often. The pool and the pole were two main reasons she wanted to move to this house. Besides the fantastic view in the front of the Vegas valley and the strip in the distance.

She slid down the pole when she saw me. "Having fun?" I asked.

"Just working up a sweat before I attack the pool. How did your investigating go? Catch the killer yet?" She was moving toward the pool but stopped long enough for me to answer.

Pasta Murders

"Take your dip, and I'll tell you everything later," I said as Willy squirmed in my arms. I knew what he wanted. I put him down, and he followed Penny into the pool. I laughed remembering back when I threw him in to learn to swim. He loved the water now, and it was hard to get him out most of the time.

Penny did a couple of laps back and forth as I sat on the plastic chairs and watched Willy trying to keep up. She finally slid up on the cement and pulled Willy up next to her. He shook, splashing everything near him. Penny laughed and stood, coming towards me. I knew what she was going to do. She plopped down on my lap getting me wet."

"Want a lap dance, big boy?" she asked.

"I think you're too late. I'm already wet," I said with a smirk.

"That's nasty. Now tell me about your day." She wiggled a little just for effect as I related everything that happened after I left her that morning.

"Oh, and the best part is, there was a review for Angelo's restaurant, and it was good." I reached over to where I set the paper and held it away from her wet body so she could see it.

She read it then she let out her little squeal, saying it was good. "I'll take it to Angelo to let him read it," she said.

"When?"

"Now. He's in the guesthouse resting. You did invite him to visit."

"Yes, I forgot. I didn't think he'd agree. Sure, let's go give him this good news. Maybe cheer him up." I stood, pushing Penny off my lap. She put on the robe she had brought out, and we went through the gate to the guesthouse on the side.

I knocked on the door. Angelo opened it a few moments later. "Hey, big guy, got some good news," I said.

"You caught the killer?" he asked.

"No, sorry, but Horn emailed in his review last night before he was killed. It's in the paper today." I handed him the folded paper, and he read it.

"Wow, come on in. This is really great. He did like the place. Wow, I have to send a copy of this to mom. She'll be pleased."

We went inside and sat in the small living area. Angelo read the article again, grinning from ear to ear. "This is so good," he said again. "I'll have to blow this up and put it in the lobby."

"That's a good idea. Now that everyone knows about your place and Horn's murder, you should have a lot of curiosity seekers. Not that you want morbid guests, but they have to eat," I said.

"I'm getting over it. I've seen enough killings in my days with the family. It was the bad press the restaurant would get from this that bothered me. But with this article, it may be salvageable."

"That's good. Now are you going to re-open?" Penny asked.

"You bet, Mrs. R. I'll probably go in tomorrow and get it ready. I'll have to call all my employees and get them in, too. How did your investigation of Horn go?"

"Yeah, there's a lot to tell," I said and told him of the day I had with Deacon and Lynn. He sat listening until I finished.

"Worked for the government? Maybe that's what happened. Someone tortured him in my restaurant to get him to talk. But why my restaurant? They could have done it in his apartment," Angelo said.

"Yep, I said that, too. It doesn't make sense. There's more to this than we know, but time will tell. We'll find out eventually, and everything will be explained."

"You hope," Penny threw in.

"Thank you, my dear. I am a master detective, up there with Sam Spade, Mike Hammer and…"

"Inspector Clouseau," Penny added.

I just stared at her as Angelo laughed his head off.

*

Chapter 12

"Are you saying that I'm a bumbling, inept detective?" I asked her as she sat smiling coyly up at me.

"No, you're not bumbling," she replied with a bigger smile.

"I'm just going to ignore you," I said and turned back to Angelo. "Now are you feeling better about this review thing?"

"Oh, much better. This is a good review, and I'm sorry for the circumstances, but at least one good thing came out of it."

"Good, now I need to go in and rest," I said and turned to Penny. "You can go drown in the pool."

I reached down and picked up Willy who had planted himself at Angelo's feet. "Enjoy your evening Angelo," I said and went out. Penny followed, snickering all the way.

I stopped just before the back gate and said, "You have a show to do in the morning. Why don't you do something about Angelo's restaurant? Maybe ask him to come in and talk about what happened. It might help his business."

She looked at me in silence for a moment then said, "That's not a bad idea. We just won't mention he died being stuffed with pasta." She laughed and went past me through the gate.

I looked down at Willy still in my arms and said, "Don't ever get married."

We went into the back yard again and Penny was already in the pool. Willy, seeing that, squirmed in my arms, and I put him down. He charged to the pool and dove in.

I went back by the Greek statue and into the house. I headed towards the couch in the living room where I planned to take a quick nap, assuming Penny stayed outside long enough.

About forty minutes later my cell phone buzzed. It was Deacon. I tried to sit up but my legs were asleep so I just lay there.

"Hey, Deacon, what's up?"

Pasta Murders

"Just got word from Warren. Higgs expired about twenty minutes ago. The doctors can't figure why. He wasn't in any real danger while in his coma. I got Joe Lange going over to take the body and autopsy it. This is really strange."

"Hmm, maybe someone decided to finish the job. You, my friend, have a real mystery."

"Well, that's why I'm a detective. I solve these things," he replied.

"Keep me up to date on your detecting. How's Lynn?"

"She's resting. Still feeling sick, not sure why, so close to the baby's arrival. She should be over the sick part of it. I may reschedule her doctor's appointment for tomorrow just to be sure all is well."

"Better to be safe than sorry. Keep me informed," I said and hung up.

I was still prone on the couch when a head popped over the back and looked down at me with a smile. "Are you going to lie there all day? It's almost time for bed, and you have to go into the office in the morning to make sure it's being run properly," Penny said.

"I can't move, my legs are useless," I said.

"Along with most of your body," she said with a grin. "If you want some quick action, I'll be in bed and awake for twenty minutes. You have one minute to take advantage of the situation. That's about all you're good for." She disappeared from the back of the couch, and I struggled to get up.

I massaged my legs, and they started to function again. Standing carefully, I toddled to the bedroom.

Bob Moats

Penny was already in bed. Damn, she could move fast when she wanted to. I undressed in record time and went to take advantage of the one minute. But with my legs still half asleep, it took two minutes.

I woke early the next morning feeling better than the night before. Penny had gone to her private bathroom and was getting ready to go play TV hostess. I went to my bathroom, still a mess, and got ready for the day.

I went out to the kitchen and got my two pieces of bread to toast as Penny wolfed down her instant oatmeal. "So are you going to have Angelo on today?" I asked.

"I already called the studio and talked to Gordy. He said it was fine with him. It was recent news so it's a good subject. I went out and asked Angelo if he wanted to come on, and he was delighted. He said he wanted a copy of the show to send back home, since my show isn't national now."

"Good, any publicity is good publicity. I'm still going to see about the billboards and taxi tops. I'm sure Angelo is the talk of the town now that Horn bought it in his restaurant."

Penny looked up at the clock and stood. "I'm running late," she said and kissed me, then headed out. I glanced at Willy standing, waiting for a piece of toast. I obliged him and then got up from the snack bar.

"Shall we go in and see if Lacey is back from vacation?" I asked Willy. He wagged his tail and followed me to the front door. I picked him up, and we went out to the van.

Pasta Murders

We arrived at the office and parked in the back. I went in the back door, setting off the cowbell Lacey had attached to the door months ago. I seemed to frighten her popping in unannounced, so she made sure that wouldn't happen again.

I waved to the security camera figuring she was watching me. Willy ran down the hallway to the doggy door we'd had installed so we didn't have to keep opening the door for him to go from the front to the back.

I came to the glass doors and into the inner lobby where Lacey had her desk and the file cabinets she used to run the office. A fairly attractive woman in her thirties stood at the counter. I smiled to Lacey where she stood on the other side of the counter. She grinned at me and announced, "Jim, this is Carol Jenkins. She says she's your daughter."

I was more than a little shocked to hear this, and it must have shown on my face.

The woman turned to me and said, "I'm sorry if I startled you, Mr. Richards, but I'd like to talk to you about my mother, Laura Jenkins."

That was the second shock of the day. I wondered if there would be more and if my head was up to it. I did know Laura Jenkins. We'd dated about thirty years ago. "Uh, yes, I knew your mother. Please Carol, come into my office." I led her through the doors to my office and asked her to sit.

"I hope your receptionist wasn't too forward, announcing it like that," she said with a smile that reminded me of Laura. Her face wasn't too far off, either.

"Lacey likes to tell me things she knows will shake me up. Now I need an explanation."

"Of course. My mother, Laura Jenkins, passed away last year of cancer. After she was buried, I cleaned her apartment. I was going through the boxes of belongings she kept in her storage unit and found a diary she wrote in years ago. Around the time I was born."

Shock three of the day. Laura was deceased. I had cared for Laura a lot, but we weren't destined to get married or even to stay together. She wasn't ready to settle down with me, so we decided to separate. I lost track of her. It would have been too hard to stay close. I married after we split and then divorced five years later, after my son was born. Damn, I'd have to tell my son he had a sister.

"I'm really sorry to hear about Laura. She was quite a woman. I suppose the diary told you about me?"

"Somewhat, yes. Before I read the diary, she never mentioned you or who my real father was all these years. She married a man when I was about twelve, but he wasn't much of a father figure. They lasted about two years and then divorced. He wasn't a very nice person. I asked her about my real father, and she said he ran off, leaving her alone with me."

That didn't set well with me. "I never ran off from your mother, and I never knew about you. We broke up because she wasn't ready to settle down. I asked her to marry me, but she refused. She was very independent and free willed."

"Yes, her diary explained some of that. She said didn't want to burden my father with the obligation of a daughter, or so she wrote."

"That's crazy. I asked her to marry me. I would have loved knowing I had a daughter. This is all happening so fast. I'm sorry you had to find out this way."

"It's all right. I lost a mother, but hope I found a father. She never mentioned you were my father. She didn't even put that in her diary, but the time line of events and the lack of her saying she was with another man after you puts it about right. I was born nine months after you and mom split."

"Please understand. I don't take anything on words alone. I think we would need to have DNA tests so you'll be sure to know definitely if I'm your father."

"I feel the same way. I'm willing to take the test."

"Good. Do you know anything about what I do?"

"I know you're a private investigator and a well-known writer."

"I also have friends in the Las Vegas police department, and I think I could get their forensics people to help with the testing. Would that be alright with you?"

She agreed.

Now I would have to tell Penny. That would be an interesting conversation. Hey honey, I have some news to tell you. Oh, boy.

*

Chapter 13

I sat for a moment taking in the shock of it all. I never thought about the implications of getting a woman I was involved with pregnant. Or having a daughter. Not that I was upset, I always took things calmly and wanted proof of what was going on. Whenever there was a problem, I wanted facts. It's the way I was.

I looked at this woman and wanted to believe her unconditionally as my daughter, but that was not me. This whole situation reminded me of one of those Lifetime movies, a man discovers he has a long lost daughter and has to deal with it. Or that ABBA movie where the girl has to figure out which of three men is her father. If she was my daughter, it would be a shame that I couldn't have been there for her all these years.

"I'm sorry if I seem too calm, but I just want to make sure that you're not disappointed that I may not be your father," I said.

"I understand. I don't want to be claiming you're my dad if you aren't. It's a lot to take in. I hoped that I would find out you were. It would relieve me of all the years of wondering who my biological father was. I never had a father growing up. My mother had trouble settling down with any man. Even the man she married wasn't enough for her. He was not a nice person, but mom wasn't one to settle for one man. Which is why I need proof that you are my father."

"I understand. Laura was a wild child. I always called her that. She grew up in the sixties and stayed

85

there. I don't expect you to understand. It was the hippie revolution, and I didn't take to it well. Your mother loved it, to be free and open with life. I wanted to settle down and raise a family. Your mother wanted to save the whales and raise vegetables in an organic garden. We didn't mesh very well."

"I grew up in that environment, mom always spouting the healthy way of living. I hated it, but I put up with it."

"So, tell me about yourself."

She smiled and said, "I was born in Mt. Clemens General Hospital and spent the first five years of my life moving from place to place. Luckily, I was too young to understand. Mom just couldn't settle in one place. Her income was never great so we were forced to move most of those times."

"What did she do for a living?" I asked, hoping she wasn't turning tricks.

"She worked at a couple restaurants as either a waitress or hostess. She made better tips as a waitress. It was the only thing she enjoyed. Working around food and helping people."

"I can't imagine her slinging burgers, what with her opinions on slaughtered animals for food."

"She was actually something of a hypocrite. She spouted healthy foods but would eat meat whenever it was available. I ended up following her in her footsteps, becoming a waitress. She always helped me get a job."

Interesting, I thought. Maybe I could get her a job with Angelo's restaurant. I'd talk to him about it later.

"You came all the way here from Michigan?" I asked.

"Yes, I had a small inheritance from Mom's insurance, after burial, and used it to come here."

"How did you find me?" I asked.

"I got your name from the diary and did some exploring. I Googled you and found out a lot about you. You were mentioned regarding the Classmate Murders in Michigan and the TV movie about that case. I discovered that you moved to Las Vegas, and it wasn't hard to find you here."

I was feeling proud that she was a good detective in finding me. Maybe I should hire her to work here. Maybe I should wait for the DNA tests before I got her too stirred up.

"Where are you staying?"

"I'm in a motel off the airport for now. It was where the taxi driver took me."

"Nonsense, I have a guesthouse. You can stay there for now," I said, knowing Angelo was returning to his apartment. "I'll take you to the motel so you can get your things and then take you to my home."

"I don't want to put you out, please."

"Carol, if you are my daughter, you are more than welcome to use the guesthouse. Even if you're not, you are Laura's daughter, and I can't have you staying in some flea bag motel. No argument, we will go get your things." I stood, came around the desk and took her hand. It was soft like her mother's. I gave myself a mental shake. I was being ridiculous. I couldn't remember how her hand had felt so long ago.

Carol followed me out to the front as I told Lacey we'd be back. Lacey gave me her evil eye, and I told her to pull it back in. We went to the back door, and she followed me to the van.

"This is nice, a person could live in here," she said admiring the van.

"It's a Class B motorhome, meant for camping but a person could live in it. Before I got into being a private investigator and married my wife, I had dreams of living in one of these. Now we just go camping in it."

"I'm sure you must have felt mom was a gypsy somewhere in a past life. She always wanted to move around."

I drove out of the parking lot and asked where she was staying. She told me the name. I knew the motel from past investigations. "When I was with your mother, she wasn't too much into traveling, but she always talked about it. It must have been hard moving around with a baby."

"She'd wrap me up, put me in the stroller, and we'd be off again. I don't remember any of it, but she made sure I knew about it."

"Laura was a kind, gentle woman. She would have made sure you were taken care of," I said as I pulled up to the motel parking lot. She got out, and I followed her to her room. She gathered her few items and put them in an old suitcase. I took the suitcase. She left the key on the table, and closed the door.

Bob Moats

"Should I go see if I can get a refund on my room for the days I'm not going to be here?" she asked as we walked to the van.

"Don't even bother. If you need money, I'll take care of it." I guess I felt a little guilty that I didn't provide for her all those years.

Next I needed to get her into the guesthouse and explain to Penny why there was an attractive woman living there. It was different when I brought home Jessie, the little girl whose father was killed by the Vegas Vigilante. Then we let Lacey live with us while I tried to help her figure out if she murdered a man. But this woman was older, and I had to explain that she might be my daughter. Penny is easygoing and takes life as it comes, but this would be a surprise. Besides, she would never let me live it down.

"Do you know anything about my wife, Penny Wickens?" I asked, opening the side van door so we could put her suitcase inside.

"Of course, I used to watch her show back in Michigan. Then when she went to the CW network, I watched that show, also. I'm looking forward to meeting her."

"Well, you will soon," I said. My cell phone buzzed. I glanced at the caller ID. It was Deacon. "Excuse me, I have to take this." I moved over to the sidewalk as Carol got in the van. "Hey, guy, I've got some news and a favor to ask. But you called me. What do you need?"

"Joe Lange did the autopsy and a prelim tox. Higgs was poisoned. Probably through the IV he had.

89

Pasta Murders

We have another murder, I hope the last. Are you available today? Lynn is not feeling well. I got her an appointment today with her doctor, and Warren is going to drive her in. She insisted I go investigate Higgs' murder."

"I'm having a situation myself today. I just found out I may have a daughter I didn't know about. I may need your help getting a DNA test."

"A daughter? Trying to show me up? How old is this girl? Does Penny know about this?"

"Stop with the questions! She's in her thirties, not sure how old exactly. I just found out about an hour ago, so I'll have more details for you later. Can you arrange a DNA test?"

"Sure, I'll talk to forensics and see if they can rush it through, but you know it's not a fast test."

"Thanks. I need to get this woman into my guesthouse and talk to Penny when she's done with her show today. I'm wondering how that will go."

"Knowing Penny, I think she'll take it well," Deacon said. I could tell he was enjoying this.

"I'm not worried about her accepting it. I'm concerned she'll make me miserable for the rest of my life about the fact of having a previously unknown daughter. I've never bragged about my sex life before I met her, and this will give her ammunition."

"Well, good luck. Call me when you're ready to investigate."

"I will. Thanks, and talk later." I hung up. Now on to inform Penny we have a daughter.

Chapter 14

I speed dialed Penny. I figured her show had finished taping. Her phone rang a couple times, and she answered. "Lola's love shack, how may I help you?"

She'd answered before with silly sayings, but I was taken by surprise this time. With all that was going on that day, I was speechless for a moment.

"Jim, if you're going to just breathe into the phone, I'm going to have to charge you for phone sex," she said.

"Uh, are you finished for the day?" I stammered.

"Yes, are you okay?"

"Well, I have something to tell you and you need to be at the house for me to explain. Can you go there?"

"Sure. Are you breaking up with me? I want half of everything and custody of Willy," she said with a laugh.

"No, not breaking up, just adding to the family."

"Are you bringing home another stray?" she asked.

I wasn't sure how to answer that. "Just meet me at the house. I'll explain there," I said and hung up. I probably shouldn't have hung up on her.

I went to the van, and Carol and I drove to the house. I got there first. Penny's studio was farther away than my office. I took Carol to the guesthouse. It was clean. One thing about Angelo, he respected other people's property.

Pasta Murders

"I love this tiny house. I love your house, too. Such a beautiful view of Las Vegas," she said, standing at the front doorway looking out to the valley.

"Wait until you see it at night. There should be everything in here you'll need. Clean linens are in that closet along with bed sheets. Just yell if you need anything."

"Thank you so much. This is more than I hoped for."

"Okay, just rest in here until I explain you to Penny. This may take a while."

She laughed lightly. The sound brought back memories of her mother. "I'll come and get you when it's time." I went out and to the front to wait for Penny to drive in. I sat on the porch and realized I had left Willy at the office. I'd get him later.

About five minutes later Penny drove in and parked in the drive. She came up and sat on the steps next to me. "So what is this earth shaking news? Am I going to make you pack and get out?"

"I hope not. Do you remember that ABBA movie and the play about the girl trying to find out who her father was?"

"Sure," she said.

"Well, a girl found me today. She thinks I may be her father." I waited for that to sink in.

Penny was quiet for a moment then laughed. "Oh, my God. You have a secret daughter? This is amazing. Where is she?"

"In the guesthouse. She arrived from Michigan today and came to the office."

Bob Moats

"Who and how?"

"The mother? She was an old flame of mine, so this girl could be my daughter. The timing was right, after we broke up. As to how, I'm sure you know how. She never knew who her father was, then her mother passed away last year and she found an old diary. It mentioned me, she did some figuring, and here she is. She agreed to a DNA test. There's little doubt in my mind that she could be my daughter, but I need to be 100% certain. She needs to be 100% certain."

"I can understand that. I want to meet her," Penny said easily. Maybe I wasn't going to get the works from her after all. "How old is she?"

"She's in her thirties. I didn't ask her exact age. You can do that. She's attractive like her mother was and smart like me."

"I doubt that she gets her smarts from you. Let's go meet her." Penny stood and waited for me to get up. I had sat so long on the concrete, my body was not responding fast. She pulled me up, and we headed to the guesthouse. I asked, "Did you have Angelo on the show today?"

She stopped and said, "Yes, and it was a very good show. We talked about the murder, but not in detail, and Angelo did fine telling about his restaurant and a little about his past. I was surprised he even talked about it. He did real well. Now, no more stalling, I want to meet your daughter." She went off towards the guest house. I had to hurry to keep up.

We arrived at the door, and I knocked. The door opened, and Penny grinned as Carol stood there.

93

Pasta Murders

"Mrs. Richards, so good to meet you. Or is it Wickens?"

"I hyphenate it when I'm away from the show. Good to meet you." She turned to me and waited.

"Oh, I'm sorry. Penny this is Carol Jenkins. Carol, Penny."

Penny took Carol in a hug, and said, "Well, if you're Jim's daughter, welcome to the family."

"We'll see after the test. I hope this gets resolved. I've never known a father."

Penny smiled and said, "I understand. My father passed away when I was young so I didn't know him very well. Hopefully this will all turn out good. Do you swim?"

Like clockwork, Penny slipped in the pool question. Jessie and Lacey had to go into the pool as soon as they got here. I wasn't surprised that she would get to it right off with Carol.

"I love to swim," Carol replied.

"Good. We have a big pool, and I hate swimming alone. I have extra swimsuits if you need one."

Penny had hundreds of swimsuits. One for every day of the year. Penny looked at me. "Don't you have some investigating to do? For Angelo?"

I quickly explained to Carol about the case of the food critic murder and my involvement. I apologized but had to leave.

"So go. Carol and I have some bonding to do." Penny laughed and took Carol to the house to get a swimsuit.

I stood in the guesthouse feeling alone, so I called Deacon.

A half hour later I was sitting in Lynn's office telling Deacon all about my morning. He sat back taking it all in.

"That's funny. Now Penny has another female in the household to play with. Are you still going to have the DNA testing?"

"If you can set it up. But I'm not really sure if I want to do it. I think she would be disappointed if I weren't her father. That would leave her without a mother and a father."

"Well, it's up to you two. Let me know. Now back to Higgs."

"Yes, you said Joe Lange ruled it a homicide."

"Yep, no other way the poison could have gotten into his system. Someone injected it in his IV. Joe couldn't find any puncture marks on his body."

"Why wasn't he being guarded?"

"He committed no crime, and we didn't figure he was in danger. Weber didn't authorize a guard, budget cuts and all that."

"Okay, so we're nowhere with Horn's murder and now Higgs. Maybe we should go over Horn's apartment again and then Higgs' place. We may find something."

"Right now, it's something to try. I'll call Warren to see how Lynn's check-up went, then we'll go." He picked up his cell phone and dialed Warren. "Hey Greg, how's it going at the doctor's?" He listened, made a few agreeable noises and hung up.

"Well?" I asked.

Pasta Murders

"All's well. Lynn has a small infection, nothing serious, but dragging her down. The nice thing is the doctor ordered her to bed rest until the infection goes away. It's going to kill her, but she doesn't want to hurt the baby."

"And you'll rest easier knowing she's off the force for now."

"Yes, I got my wish. Now shall we go scope out the apartments?"

We drove back to the towers and into security again. Daniel Keller greeted us, and we asked to see the apartment again.

"How is Mr. Higgs doing? I heard he was in a car crash?"

"Sorry, but he passed on this morning. You now have two apartments to resell. We'll also need to see Higgs' apartment."

Keller looked stunned at the news of Higgs' death. Then he composed himself and took us up to Horn's apartment first. He used his door card, and we went in. I noticed that the crime scene tape was gone. Keller probably removed it for the sake of the other residents.

We spent about an hour looking around. CSI had gone over it for evidence, but they weren't investigating for anything that Horn might have hidden that was important enough to murder two people for.

I was looking at the old Remington typewriter that sat on the desk. The newspaper editor said Horn carried that machine throughout his career. I turned it over. There was nothing on the bottom but the manufacturer's label. I set it back down. It was heavy. I went through the desk drawers and found nothing.

"Have you found any relatives for Horn?" Deacon asked Keller.

"He had a sister in Maine. We contacted her and she said to just dump everything. Sad, a life just tossed out."

I looked around the room. There was a lot of good stuff still there. Furniture and nice art objects. "Mr. Keller, let me make arrangements to clean out the place. I'll contact you in a day or two if that's all right."

"The rent's paid until the end of the month, so that will be fine."

We dug around some more but found nothing of importance. "Why are you volunteering to clean out this place?" Deacon asked me.

"I have my reasons," I said.

*

Chapter 15

"How much is the rent on these apartments?" I asked in the elevator on the way up to Higgs' apartment.

Keller smiled and said, "There's no rent, Mr. Richards. People buy the apartments outright, but they do pay a monthly maintenance fee."

"If I knew someone who wanted to buy Horn's apartment, what would it run?"

Pasta Murders

"His apartment was close to three million dollars. The monthly maintenance fee is $950.00 and payable every six months."

I looked at Deacon and gave him an eye roll. "Sure, chump change," I said. The elevator stopped on the floor two up from Horn. We got off, and Keller led us to a door. "You're sure Higgs is dead?" he asked.

"I know a dead guy when I see one. Besides, he's been autopsied. I don't think if he were alive, he'd like that."

"I'm sorry, I just wanted to be sure before I let you enter." He used his card, and the locks released. He turned the handle and opened the door. There was a strange smell coming from the apartment. Deacon recognized it, decomp.

"Mr. Keller, wait out here." He drew his weapon and went in. I followed, holding my nose. I was surprised the neighbors didn't smell this.

Deacon walked through the place until he got to the bathroom. He opened the door and almost choked. The body in the tub was unrecognizable. It was almost beyond decomposing. He closed the door and told me to get out. He followed and closed the entrance door, pulling out his cell phone. He called for back-up and CSI. He reported to dispatch that he was at a crime scene.

Keller looked pale. He asked, "Is it bad?"

"Well, if you don't clean the bathroom, you may need to seal this apartment and take a loss," Deacon said, smiling wryly at Keller's discomfort.

About a half hour later the place was overrun with cops and forensic people. The hallway was becoming a gathering place for residents who wanted to know what was going on. Only the smell was keeping them at a distance.

Joe Lang came out. "I haven't had a good decomp in a long while. This one will be a challenge to identify. His teeth are missing, and his hands were cut off. He's naked, and no ID. So it will be a challenge." He smiled and walked back into the room. A few minutes later, the body bag came out with the EMTs pulling the gurney.

"So, this is getting deep," Deacon said to me. "It looks like Horn and Higgs had something in common. Why would someone leave a body in Higgs' apartment? A warning? Or maybe Higgs did this and was getting ready to dissect the body, but he was delayed by his accident."

"We still haven't explored the apartment," I said.

"When CSI clears it, we'll take over. So how did Penny handle finding out about your indiscretion?"

My indiscretion? I see you're still using that word improvement book Lynn gave you. Penny took it better than I expected. She took Carol right to the pool, so all is well. Now to have the test to see if she's really my daughter."

"If she hadn't agreed to the test, I'd say maybe she was a con artist scamming you for your money."

"But she did agree, so I believe her." Joe Lang came past us and smiled, then continued on, following the body.

99

Pasta Murders

"I can get you the test. I talked to forensics. They agreed to keep it under the radar. It's not official police business. So you need to get a mouth swab from both of you. I'll get the vials with the swabs. It will take about a week for the results. Things don't happen like they do on TV."

"That's okay. I can get to know her in that time. So can Penny."

The supervisor of the CSI team came out followed by his people. "It's okay to go in now. Just be careful."

"Thanks Bill," Deacon said and we went in. The windows in the apartment wouldn't open, so they had turned up the air conditioning to blow the smell around. It still stank. The bathroom had a ventilating fan. It was on. Someone had sprayed air freshener, and it helped a little.

Keller slowly came into the apartment, sniffing and making faces. "This is not good, break-ins, and murders. I may have to answer to the owners about this," he said, following Deacon around as he talked to him.

"Mr. Keller, you couldn't have prevented this if you tried. I believe this was professional. Government or the mob, but someone who knew what they were doing."

Keller looked at me. "Are you interested in cleaning out this apartment, too?"

I looked around. It was as nice as Horn's, maybe a little nicer. "I'll let you know. I may be interested."

Keller at least smiled hearing that. However, he was getting paler by the minute and finally excused himself, leaving the room. Deacon laughed.

"He's not exactly ready for crime fighting. He's so used to building management that he doesn't even have the nuts to handle it," Deacon said.

"I'm not seeing anything that tells me anything. I'm going to have a couple storage units to put everything in. If it comes down to it, we can explore this stuff again," I said.

"You really are going to clear this out?"

"Hey, it's free, and the furnishings are expensive. I have a plan. Whether or not Carol is my daughter, I'm going to need to set her up in a place. May as well be furnished."

"You think she'll mind having the furniture of dead men?" Deacon laughed.

"If it's free and expensive, I'll talk her into it."

There was nothing more to find. We decided to close up and leave. Keller was in the hallway looking ill.

"We're finished for now, Mr. Keller. You can close it up, and we'll be in touch," Deacon said.

"I'm going to have a moving crew to take both apartments' contents. I'll call when I can arrange it," I told the man.

"Thank you, Mr. Richards. It will make it easier to have both places cleaned."

We left and I asked, "Now where?"

"I have no idea. This is where Lynn would do her deducting, and I would follow," he said.

Pasta Murders

"This is why you bring me along. This is not the first time I've had to help you. You really need to learn how to deduce." I laughed.

"I'm your Dr. Watson to your Sherlock. So you tell me where to go."

"Sorry, I have no idea. Let me sleep on it, and we can start in the morning. I've had a long day discovering I had a new relative. Now I need to go rescue her from Penny. Oh, and I need to pick up Willy at the office and listen to Lacey interrogate me about my daughter."

"Okay, I'll drop you off and go see my poor baby. She should be home by now."

We both went out to the car and drove back to the precinct. I retrieved my van and drove back to the office. I came in the front this time and said hello to Tracey in the front lobby. She smiled as I went through the doors to the inner lobby.

Willy must have heard my voice and came running. He bounced around my feet, and I scooped him up. Lacey was sitting quietly and giving me her look. The one that said I was not being nice to her.

"Okay, welcome back, Lacey. How was your vacation?" I said.

"Very nice, now talk to me about the daughter," she said in one breath.

I smiled and put Willy on the counter. I explained the sordid details of my sordid past, and she sat nodding. "Okay, is that enough to make you happy?"

"I'll forgive you this time. You had things on your mind when you zipped out of here earlier. I would have liked to know what was going on."

"I'll remember that next time I find out I have a child. I also have a couple murders to solve. Want to hear about that?"

"No, I'm more interested in your personal life." She smiled at me from her desk.

"Is Buck in?" I asked.

"He came in about two hours ago and hasn't come out of his office."

"Thank you, Lacey. You'll really have to tell me about your vacation. But later." I took up Willy again and went to Buck's office. He was sitting back in his chair, sound asleep. I went to his desk and slammed my hand down. He came up ready to fight.

"Just like old times in my office back in Michigan," I said with a laugh.

"You're still mean," he said and sat back in his chair. "What's this I hear about you having a daughter?"

I laughed and told him about my day. He sat listening and then said, "Wow, your past is catching up to you. That's why I never gave women my real name. So they couldn't find me later on."

"Well, I was more involved with the woman than just a one night stand. As I said, I even asked her to marry me. Too bad we lost touch. I would have known about my daughter sooner."

"You don't know that. Women are funny. They do what they want even though we think we run everything. They actually have the control, and they hold our balls tightly."

"You are so right, my friend," I said thinking about Penny.

*

Chapter 16

"You seem to be taking this daughter thing lightly," Buck said.

"It's something I can't change. I accept things on faith but I also need proof, which is why we're going to be tested for DNA."

"Smart. So how's the food guy murder case going?" Buck asked, sitting back in his chair.

I put Willy down, and he skittered out of the room. Probably going back up to see Lacey. I sat on the chair in front of Buck's desk and related everything to him. "So we now have three dead bodies and nothing to go on."

"If this Horn was doing work for the government, why don't you talk to Earl and see what he can find through his connections?"

Buck had a good idea. Earl had a shady background with the government working for the CIA. He'd been involved in some black ops escapades. He could call our FBI inside man, Harold, and have him check on Horn. "Very good idea, Buck, thank you. Is Earl in his office?"

"Jimmy, you came in and found me sleeping. Do you really think I would know?" He gave me his famous walrus smile, and I laughed.

"I'll go see if he's available. You can go back to the hard work you were doing." I stood and went out and down the hallway towards Earl's office. He was in.

"Jim, you do work here," he said with a grin.

"You keep saying that. Aren't I here enough for you?"

"I don't keep tabs. What is it you need?"

"Harold."

"Ah, some clandestine report on a subject?"

I told him all about my adventures with Horn, Higgs and the mysterious body in Higgs' bathtub. Also about Horn's connection to the government.

"I know of Horn through his food and restaurant column. He died stuffed with pasta, eh? Ironic for him. I'll call Harold and see what he can come up with. I think my favors are running low, though. I'll have to bribe him with a case of good rum. Like we drank back in Tahiti on that cruise."

"I almost forgot about the mystery writer's cruise. Tahiti was fun until we were getting shot at. Let me know if Harold finds anything. I'll let Deacon know we're inquiring. Thanks," I said.

I went back out to see if I could find Willy. He liked to hide on me when I was getting ready to leave for the day. I found him under Lacey's desk. She laughed as I tried to coax him out.

"Do you want me to pick him up in the morning?" Lacey asked.

Pasta Murders

"No, my new daughter is staying in our guesthouse, and I think I'll have her watch Willy. It will be good for both her and the dog."

"Do you really think she's your daughter?"

"The test will tell. I like her so far, but really need to get to know her. It's been about thirty years that I didn't know she existed. Now I have to catch up." I picked up Willy when he finally came out, and we went to the van.

I sat in the van, called Deacon and told him about having Harold checking on Horn. He agreed it was a good idea. Maybe something in his past would come out. I hung up and started the van then drove out of the parking lot. I was thinking about what I would do with Carol. Take her out for ice cream and buy her dolls? She was a little old for that. I'd sit her down in the backyard and talk. That was what I could do first.

I finally arrived home and let Willy run to do his business on the front lawn. I heard a door open and close. It was Penny coming from the guesthouse.

"Hi, Sweetie. How was your day fighting crime?" she asked with that smile that always made my heart beat a little faster.

I filled her in as we watched Willy chase a butterfly around the bushes. She smiled and waited for me to finish.

"Now what lies about me have you been telling Carol?" I asked.

"Use your imagination. She's a delightful girl. She's had a rough life, living with her mother. That woman had to be slightly off in the head."

"I didn't want to admit that. I knew back then she was odd, but I never realized how much. I want to get to know Carol, but I want to be careful in case she isn't my daughter. I don't want to get her hopes up too high. Would you mind if she and I spent a little time alone to talk?"

"No, I had my couple hours. I learned a lot. She's fragile, so be easy. Why don't you take her to Angelo's restaurant for dinner and have your talk?"

"Is Angelo open again?"

"Yep, he called and asked if you were here. I told him you were out, and he said he opened for business today. Call him and get a nice table."

I kissed Penny on the lips and said, "Thank you, I will."

An hour later, Carol and I were seated in a private area of Momma Mia. Angelo came by to welcome us and asked if we would like a drink."

"No, my friend, we'll wait. Angelo, this is Carol Jenkins, my new daughter. Carol this is Angelo, my friend and former mob enforcer. But he's a big teddy bear when he gets to know you."

"Real nice to meet you, Carol," he said as he took her hand to shake. "Penny told me a little of the story when I called earlier."

"Yeah, she said you called. Did you need anything important?"

"Just wanted to know where I could get Horn's article blown up and framed."

"I'll take care of it for you. I know a place. I can have it for you in a day or two."

Pasta Murders

"Thanks, Mr. R. Business has been brisk today since I re-opened. Getting a lot of curiosity seekers. I roped off the table Horn was murdered at out of respect. But people all want to be near it. Strange isn't it?"

"People have a morbid sense of interest. Like slowing for a car accident."

"Yep, they do. We'll I'll let you two talk and when you're ready to order, just wave," he said and went off.

"Was he really in the mob?" Carol asked when Angelo was out of sight.

"He was. I'll tell you more about him later. First I want to get to know you better."

She gave me a nice smile and said, "Where do I start, from birth or later?"

We sat talking and finally had a meal, prepared by Angelo himself. It was delicious. We talked some more after the table was cleared. Carol did have a rough life as Penny said. She and her mother were basically poor and had to keep moving to avoid being evicted from the places they lived. Carol barely finished high school, having to move so much, but she did. Which was good.

"Have you thought about what you're going to do now?" I asked.

"Since you're so nice to let me stay in your guesthouse, I'm going to look for a job. I've been a waitress for so long, it's about all I know. I never had any formal training for anything else."

"Okay, what if I ask Angelo to see if he has a position for you here in Momma Mia?"

"I don't want you to go out of your way, but it would be nice. This is such a lovely place."

"Wait here," I said and went off to find Angelo. A few minutes later we both came back.

"So, Carol, you say you are a waitress?" Angelo asked her.

"I was back in Michigan. I worked in fast food places and a couple nicer restaurants. Not as nice as yours, though," she replied.

Angelo looked to me and said, "She knows how to B.S., I like that." He turned back to Carol. "Okay, come in tomorrow morning at nine sharp, and I'll see what we can do."

"Thank you, sir, I really appreciate it."

"First thing, my name is Angelo. Everyone calls me Angelo. So you call me Angelo, too."

"Thank you, Angelo."

"First thing in the morning, nine sharp, don't be late." He mimicked a gun with his hand and fingers then turned and walked away.

Carol's eye went wide. "He wouldn't shoot me if I were late, would he?"

"Just ignore his mannerisms. He likes to have fun," I said as I sat back down. "Now we'll have to see about getting you transportation and a GPS. This town is huge."

We finished up and went back to the house. Penny was watching TV on the couch when we came in. She handed me a beer. Such a wonderful woman. We sat talking about the restaurant and Carol getting a job there.

"You'll love working for Angelo. He's a great guy," Penny said. "Try and learn as much as you can from him. He's a wiz in the kitchen."

"I wouldn't mind cooking. I've always enjoyed it," Carol said.

"Well, let him know. He has two girls who cook for him, and maybe he'll train you, also," I said.

We watched a couple TV shows, and then Carol said, "I don't want to overstay my welcome. I'm tired, so if you don't mind, I'm going to bed."

"You do what you want. You're at home here. Good night," I said. Penny agreed.

After she left, my cell phone buzzed. The Caller ID said it was private. This late at night I wasn't sure if I wanted to answer it, but I did. It was Harold calling all the way from Washington, D.C., and he asked if I was sitting down.

*

Chapter 17

"I'm on the couch, so what is so urgent that I need to sit?" I asked.

"Alfred Horn, food and restaurant critic for the Las Vegas Review-Journal. Now deceased," Harold said.

"That much I know."

"Okay, but you didn't know much about his background in government."

"I have a feeling you'll tell me. You really love suspense, don't you?"

I could hear him chuckle, and then he continued, "Alfred Horn, GSA employee starting in 1951. Now I'm reading this from their website for your information, 'General Services Administration was established by President Harry Truman on July 1, 1949, to streamline the administrative work of the federal government. GSA consolidated the National Archives Establishment, the Federal Works Agency and its Public Buildings Administration, the Bureau of Federal Supply and the Office of Contract Settlement, and the War Assets Administration into one federal agency…' etc., etc. Horn was listed as an editor for journals and reports throughout the administration. He had access to all kinds of documents regarding government operations. He left government service in 1971 and went into a new career as a newspaper columnist."

"Okay, he was a paper pusher for boring info about the operations of the government. Anything earth shattering?"

"Yep, he took a lot of classified information about certain things the government didn't want released to the public and hid that information. The government didn't do anything to him because they had no real proof he had the documents, but they did give him such a hard time on his job that he quit. I'm surprised he didn't turn the info over to the press after the treatment he got."

"What info did he have that was so bad?"

Pasta Murders

"I couldn't find out. That's the kicker. No one is admitting to anything. The investigation about his involvement in removing classified files is a matter of public record, but the case was closed with no resolution. I tracked down a few people who were there, and they said Horn held the investigators hostage. He had damaging info, and he had safeguards in case anything happened to him. He claimed to have files hidden somewhere and someone to release the files if he turned up dead."

"Well, something happened to him, he's dead. So where are his safeguards?"

I thought of Higgs. Could he have been the safeguard? Was he supposed to release the files if Horn turned up dead? Was Horn interrogated to tell them who the safeguard was, and was that the reason Higgs was dead?

"So why would they be interested now after all these years?" I asked.

"Got me. It's an election year, and Horn hated a number of men in government who may have things to hide. Maybe they wanted to be sure he didn't spill any beans."

"Now we're getting into some weird speculation. We've established that he had something someone wanted, so he was killed for it and his apartment trashed. But did they find anything? Now this man Higgs, Horn's lover, was also killed. He could have been the safeguard."

"You're closer to the situation than I am. You'll have to find the files. But watch out, it could mean death for you, too, if you do find them. Hope this helped. I'll dig around some more. This was all I could get on short notice. Tell Earl to ship the rum soon." I heard him laugh, and he hung up.

I turned to Penny still sitting quietly on the couch and said, "This could turn out to be a political thriller, maybe my next book."

"If you write another book. You haven't finished the one about your adventures in Area 51 yet."

"I know, I'll get to it. Now we need to get some sleep. I have a lot to investigate tomorrow and something to tell Deacon. Oh, and I'll take Willy into the office, or do you want to take him with you?"

"I'll take him. He hasn't been to work with me for a while. The girls will be happy to see him. Are you driving Carol to Angelo's tomorrow?"

"I can do that. I'll need to take her out and get her a car this week. When did our lives get so busy?"

"You wanted to move here to Sin City and be a big shot detective. I protested the move, but, no, you insisted."

I stared at her for a moment, then got up and went to the bedroom. She laughed, turned off the TV and told Willy to come along. We wouldn't be having sex tonight.

The next morning I called out to Carol and asked if she was ready.

"I've been ready since seven. I'm a little nervous."

"Well, don't be. Angelo is easy to work for. He wants everything to be perfect, but he's not a mean boss. You'll do fine."

113

Pasta Murders

Penny said good-bye to us and grabbed Willy, put him in his travel bag and breezed out the door.

"You carry the dog in a purse?" Carol asked with a laugh.

"Ever since he was a pup. Easier to take him places that normally wouldn't let dogs in. But he's getting bigger now. Penny usually takes the dog carrier, easier for her to take him into her studio. Are you ready to go?"

"Ready as I'll ever be."

We went out to the van and I drove her to Angelo's. She got out and I said that Penny would pick her up later when she finished with her show. I had given Carol the cell phone numbers for both Penny and me, and she gave us hers. She thanked me and went into the restaurant. I felt like I was taking my daughter to her first job. Okay, now I could relive what I missed years ago. I headed to LVMPD and parked in back. Deacon was in the parking lot so I went over to him.

"Morning, Jim," he said.

"Just getting here?" I asked.

"Nope, I'm waiting for the Dodge Interceptor to be returned. It was supposed to be here fifteen minutes ago."

"You really like using that car, don't you?"

"It gives me a sense of power." He laughed.

"Well, I got some goodies to tell you." While we stood in the hot sun waiting for the car, I repeated everything Harold told me.

"Wow, that's interesting. So where do we take it from here?"

"We need to examine everything in Higgs' apartment again. If he was Horn's safeguard, then he must have some info about it somewhere."

"Keller is going to love us. Here comes the car now." The souped up Dodge Charger pulled in, and Detective Williams got out. I hadn't seen Williams in a while. He looked better than the last time I saw him. He'd put on more weight and was tan. I wondered if he was still a screw-up, but I wasn't going to ask that.

"Did you put gas into it?" Deacon asked.

"Yep, filled it up. It's all yours now. Hey, Jim, how are you doing?" he asked.

"Good to see you again. I'm doing well, thanks," I said as Williams handed the keys to Deacon.

"Later guys," he said and went off. We got in the car, and Deacon tore out of the lot and on to the highway. I always noticed a change in Deacon when he was behind the wheel of that car.

We ended up back at the towers and went in to see Keller. He wasn't in, and the man taking his place gave us a hard time about getting into the apartment. Deacon had to give him a push, reminding him it was still a crime scene and he was the primary detective.

"I could call your boss and bother him to let us in," Deacon growled.

The man stammered a bit then took us up to Higgs' apartment. That elevator ride was really quiet.

We went through the apartment again, tearing into everything we could examine. I even looked into vases with dried flowers in them. After an hour and half of searching, we had found nothing

Pasta Murders

"So if Higgs was the safeguard, he must have had the location of the files in his head. They aren't in the apartment," I said, wearing down.

"We need to find out if Horn or Higgs had a storage unit somewhere," Deacon said.

"How would you do that?"

"Easy, I'll assign Williams to call all the storage companies in town and see if he can find one they rented. I always love giving Williams the grunt work."

We thanked Keller's assistant and left the building. "Are you still taking the contents of the apartments?"

"Thanks for reminding me. I'll have to call a mover, and I'll need a storage unit, too. Interesting twist."

"I'll see if Williams can find the storage place, and you can kill two birds with one stone."

We were back at the car when Deacon's cell phone rang. He answered and listened for a minute, then hung up. We both got in the car, and he turned to me. "The man in the tub was murdered by what Joe Lang believes was an ice pick to the back base of the head. Right through the brain. Ouch." He started the car and drove out of the parking lot. "Still no ID on the body. Joe is working on something he hopes will pan out. Seems the body had a tattoo on his right arm. It was a swastika, Nazi type. Remember what Higgs said about Nazis harassing Horn?"

"I wonder if Higgs caught one of them and killed him. Maybe he was going to cut up the man to dispose of the corpse, but his accident prevented him from finishing."

"It's a thought. Now we have to track down the Nazis and see if they're missing a member."

*

Chapter 18

"Did you have Warren run down Higgs' or Horn's financials?" I asked.

"No, not yet, but I will," Deacon replied.

"I was thinking, Horn was a famous newspaper columnist but I doubt he earned enough at the R-J to buy and pay for his apartment," I said, "and do you know what Higgs did to make big bucks?"

"Are you asking or going to tell me?" Deacon said with a smile.

"Asking. Something to check on along with the financials. Do I have to do all your work for you?"

"It would be nice, relieve me of all the responsibility or blame."

"That's all I'm good for, I know. When are you getting the swabs for the DNA test?"

"Work, work, work. That's all you want me to do. I got them before you arrived today." He reached into his jacket pocket and pulled out two tubes containing the swabs. "Be sure to label which is yours and which is hers. My friend in the lab said he'd put a rush on it."

"Thanks, Deacon. I'll do it tonight and get them to you tomorrow." I put them in the pocket of my sport coat and sat back as Deacon tried to zip down Las Vegas Boulevard, AKA "the Strip." He was catching every red light. I had to smile as he grumbled about having to stop at each corner.

We arrived back at the precinct, and Deacon parked the car safely behind the building, under some palm trees barely providing shade. We went in, and Deacon found Greg Warren at his desk in the squad room.

"Greg, can you do that magic you do and get Horn's and Higgs' financials?" Deacon asked the detective. "They were living in very expensive digs on little salary. Oh, and find out what Higgs did that he could make enough money to live in the towers."

"I'll get on it right away," Warren replied. Deacon came back to me in Lynn's office.

"Now, how could the two of them afford to live in the money towers?" he asked.

"Blackmail? Maybe Horn was blackmailing someone with the information he had," I replied.

"That's good, easy money for little work. He probably set his lover up, also. It would be too obvious if they lived together."

"From the hints Harold, who likes to be cryptic, was dropping, I get the feeling this is politically motivated. Some big shot politician with a shady past is running for office, and Horn was not happy with that. The politician was not happy paying out, so he had a hit out on Horn. Then he found out Higgs was his safeguard and had him taken out, too."

"As good a theory as any. But how does the Nazi in the bathtub fit into this?" he asked.

"Got me. We need to find a few good Nazis in town and ask. Do you know any?" I asked with a grin.

"No, but I know who might." He reached for the desk phone and dialed a number. He waited a moment and then said, "Larry, it's Deacon. Have a minute for a couple questions?" He listened again. "Sure, we can come over. Give us a few." He hung up, then said to me, "I have a friend in the Gang Unit. I'm sure he'd know. Shall we take a walk?"

I followed him through the building to another squad room filled with men dressed in various biker gang colors along with a number of men in either t-shirts or suits. Deacon headed to one cubicle and looked in.

The man seated in the cubicle saw him and said, "Deacon, have you been hiding from me? You've missed two poker nights. I want your money." The man laughed.

"Sorry, Larry, I have to save for the baby. It's due in a couple months."

"Congratulations. I hope it doesn't look like you. Now what can I do for you?"

"Nazis," Deacon said, then waited.

Larry looked at me. "Richards, are you and Deacon changing sides now? Going to Der Fuhrer's camp?"

"We may have a dead Nazi in a bathtub, and we need to identify him," I said.

"You have a mug shot?" he asked.

Deacon looked at me. "I don't think he had much of a face, do you?"

119

Pasta Murders

"Not enough left to get a good photo," I replied.

"Okay, how about prints or dental records? Don't you guys in homicide do your job?"

"He was missing both hands and teeth. He was also naked and had no ID. Now we need to find a few good Nazis and ask if they're missing a storm trooper.

Larry laughed and stood, yelling over the cubicle, "Marino, you over there?"

Another head popped up above another cubicle wall and said, "Yo!"

"Come on over and join us," he requested of the head. The man came out and over to us.

"What be yo request?" the man asked. He was a very dark black man with a good build under his t-shirt.

"You had a run in last year with a couple skinheads, didn't you?" Larry asked.

"Sho did, they wanted to hang my black ass. I kicked theirs first, though. Whatcha need to know?"

"You have any info on their organization? Deacon is thinking of joining."

Marino looked at Deacon and said, "I always knew your big white ass was wanting to goose step." He laughed and held out his hand. Deacon shook it. "How's Lynn doing? Still pregnant?"

"Getting close to busting, Morris. How's Althea?"

"Still sassy and running my life. Now why do you want to fool with the Aryans?"

"Got a dead Nazi, and we need to identify him."

"Got a mug shot?"

"This is going to be one of those days," Deacon said to me.

Larry laughed and said, "There wasn't much to ID on the vic's body."

"So how do you know he was one of them?" Marino asked.

"Joe Lang found a tattoo of a swastika on his arm. We just assumed he was one of the brothers."

"Don't go calling Nazis brothers. My brothers may take offence. What kind of swastika was it?"

"I didn't see it. Joe told me over the phone."

"Ah, calling in your cases now. Leg work is out for you?"

"I'm a busy man. I have to solve crime even over the phone."

"Okay, have Joe email a copy of the tattoo and I'll look into it for you. See what local tribe of Nazis he was with."

"Will do. Call whether or not you find anything," Deacon said.

Deacon and I finished up with the gang unit boys and went back to Lynn's office.

"So have you bonded with your new daughter?" Deacon asked.

"Yeah, she's had a rough life. But I hope I can help her. I got a job for her at Angelo's restaurant, and I'll need to get her a car this week," I said.

"I have about sixteen years before I have to get a car for my girl. I think I'll even hold off until she's twenty."

Warren came to the door looking happy. Deacon asked, "You got the financial already?"

Pasta Murders

"Yep, I had to really dig. Horn hid the money in a couple banks. It was so much the bank had to report that amount to the IRS, so Horn was spreading the wealth." He put a couple sheets of paper in front of Deacon. "Here's the accounting that I could get."

Deacon read over the info and whistled low. "Wow! Horn had some funds. He's worth, or was worth a couple million easily. If this is all," he said, grinning. He looked up at me. "He had to be getting this from someone. Or he had a rich family member die."

"Maybe he saved his pennies all these years."

"Or robbed a few European banks during the second War and stashed the cash in steamer trunks, moving it around until he settled in Vegas," Deacon said, looking again at the paper.

"You have a good imagination. Now use it to solve this case," I said, holding in a laugh.

"Greg, did you find out if Higgs had any side jobs?"

"Oh, yeah, that's interesting. Higgs had an escort service for gay men. Called 'Gentlemen's Agreement,' and he had some high priced clients, judging from the info I got. Don't know any names, but I was told there are a few prominent men who don't want their names involved."

"Interesting. Could he have been blackmailing those clients?" Deacon asked.

"Not if he wanted to stay in business. Or live to tell," I said.

"Which he didn't. This is getting deep." Deacon turned to me. "Shall we go see if we can get an escort for the night?"

"Oh, now you're a gay Nazi." I laughed. "What will I find out next? You're actually a woman dressing as a man?"

"I had a confusing childhood." He laughed and stood. "Greg, do you have the address of the gentleman's club?"

"No office or club, just a phone number, but I did get the address where the number went to." He handed Deacon a slip of paper and went back out to the squad room.

"Shall we pretend we're married and want to swing?" I asked.

"You swing. I'm showing my badge and busting some heads." Deacon laughed aloud and went out of the office. I followed.

As he headed back to the Charger, I said, "You know they won't tell us anything. Can you get a warrant?"

He stopped and made a call. He talked to someone and hung up. "Warrant will be delivered to the address on this paper. Now let's look tough and get us an escort."

I smiled and followed him to the muscle car. He walked with a macho swagger.

*

Chapter 19

We arrived at the address on the paper Warren gave us. The building was a nondescript apartment complex in Paradise. To explain, Paradise is the unincorporated name of an area where part of Las Vegas claims to be. The strip and most of the casinos are actually in Paradise, but the Post Office uses Vegas as their address. Less complicated. When I first lived there, I told people back in Michigan that I lived in Vegas, but, truth be known, I lived in Paradise, Nevada. If you look on any number of maps you can see Paradise is listed.

We parked and waited for a patrol car to deliver the warrant. "This is strange. With all the money they had, why use an apartment to run the business?" Deacon asked.

"If they got busted for fronting gay prostitution, it's easier to start over. Maybe?" I offered.

"True, it would save on renting an office, too. Apartments are less expensive. Here comes the warrant." He got out of the car as two patrol cars pulled in. He waved to the lead car, and they got out and came over to us.

"Okay, guys, we have a gay escort service running out of this building. We need to check it out for a homicide case I'm working and for illegal activities."

People assume prostitution is legal in Las Vegas. Not so. Clark County bans it, although it's legal in a number of counties out of Vegas. Doesn't matter if it's female sex or male sex. So Higgs' operation would be illegal here in the city.

Deacon and the officers went up to Apartment 8A and knocked. A couple seconds went by, then the door opened and a young man stood there, looking shocked at all the police.

"Sir, I have a warrant to search the premises. Please step outside," Deacon recited from memory after doing this many times.

One of the officers took the young man's arm and gently pulled him outside. The man looked fragile enough to break. Deacon entered into what would have been the living room and found eight small desks with computer monitors on each. There were only five men at the desks, each talking on a phone.

"Alright, guys, this is a bust. Everybody stand and move to the door where these officers will escort you into the parking lot for a bus to pick you up," Deacon intoned, obviously reciting a frequently-spoken command again.

I stood just outside the door and watched the men all quietly stand then move through the door. They all looked young, averaging around 16 or 17, I estimated. This was getting worse, could involve child endangerment. Too bad Higgs wasn't around.

After they all were escorted to the lot and their hands bound by plastic ties, I entered the room. Deacon and one of the officers walked around looking in the other rooms for any surprises. They found none.

Pasta Murders

"Looks clean other than this room," Deacon said as he stood staring at the desks. He picked up a ledger from one of the desks and studied it. I stood beside him and read as he held the book. There were notations with dates and times and what I assumed were code names for the clients. No real names. That would be too dangerous to leave available.

"I'll have CSI pack everything up and take it in for examination. I'm not interested in this operation. I'll give Vice a shot at it. I just wanted to find out what Higgs was up to," Deacon said as he set the book back down.

"Well you found out. Do you think Higgs or Horn may have used this information for blackmail?" I asked.

"It's a possibility. But like you said earlier, it would be a dangerous move to blackmail clients. Horn was murdered first, and I don't feel this had anything to do with it. We still have the dead Nazi and Horn's shady past. I think we need to find out more about the body in the tub first."

"So we become Nazi hunters now?" I asked with a big grin.

"Ya vole, mine froynd," Deacon said in a lousy German accent then called Vice.

A half hour later, Deacon explained the bust to a detective in Vice then turned to me. "Nick is going to keep me informed if they find anything that links to my case. I hope Marino has the photo of the tattoo and knows something about it. Otherwise I have no idea how to go about locating Nazis."

"Are we finished here?" I asked.

"Yea, Nick can have this bust. Let's go get something to eat. All this work is making me hungry."

I agreed, and we left. We ended up at Del Taco, not my first choice, but Deacon was driving. We sat in the small dining area and munched our burritos and fries as we made small talk. Deacon's cell phone buzzed, and he answered.

He listened for a minute, wrote something in his pocket notebook and hung up. He smiled and said, "That was Marino. Got a name and location of the head Nazi of the group that is associated with the swastika on the dead guy's arm."

"I'm not crazy about meeting modern day Nazis. I've seen them in the documentaries on cable. They can be a little fanatical," I said.

"Well, we're only going to talk to one of them. Marino also said that Joe sent him a photo of the vic after Joe reconstructed the face on the computer. He's going to send it to the car's communications terminal. Maybe it will help identify the man."

We went to the car and found the photo in the tray of the fancy fax that the cars all had now. We studied the face. It wasn't pretty but it was recognizable as a face. Joe loved the lab equipment CSI had and, even though he was the coroner, he loved to play with their toys.

"This may help. Let's go find out." Deacon started the car after checking the address of the home of our person of interest.

We drove over to the house which sat in a secluded part of North Vegas, parked and went to the front door. Deacon knocked, and we waited. Finally a man opened the door and frowned.

"What the hell do you people want now? I haven't broken any laws that I know if. You're always harassing me for my beliefs."

"Hold up a little. We're not here to arrest you. We just need to find out if a dead man we found is a friend of yours," Deacon said quickly before the man could close the door.

The man gave us a blank stare. "Dead man? What are you talking about?"

Deacon held out the photo. "Does this face look familiar?"

The man suddenly turned pale. "Oh, shit, that's Louis! What happened?"

"That's what we're trying to find out. He was found dead in a bathtub in an apartment owned by Taylor Higgs. Does that name sound familiar?"

The man perked up. "Yeah, Louis was giving Higgs a hard time, for personal reasons."

"Like the fact he was gay?" I asked.

"No, because he was harassing us. He hated our group. He was Jewish and blamed us for the holocaust. Hell, I wasn't there. I had nothing to do with it."

"But your people did. The Nazis were responsible," Deacon said.

"That was Hitler's folly. We're Neo-Nazis, and we have a peaceful agenda. Hell, the Klan murdered more blacks than we ever have. We never murder people. Where's Higgs now? I'd like to have a talk with him."

"He's chilling in the morgue with your friend Louis. You wouldn't know who may have murdered him?"

The man looked spooked now. "No, I don't, and I had nothing to do with it. Anything else you need to know before I go back to my TV?"

"Just your friend Louis' full name and the address where he lived."

"Hold on," he said and went back into this house. A few minutes later he returned with an index card. It had the information Deacon asked for.

"Just remember, I cooperated with you," he said and slammed the door.

"That was rude," I said.

"Yep, those Nazis can be rude." He looked at the card. "Shall we take another ride?"

We were back on the road when my cell phone buzzed. "Never a dull moment. What did we do before cell phones?" I asked rhetorically, then answered the thing. It was Penny.

"Hey, doll, what's happening?"

"I'm at Angelo's restaurant, and he's really happy with Carol. She's doing very well," Penny bubbled over the phone. "Angelo said he may train her for kitchen work, if she wants. I'm going to visit with him for a while then take her home. She doesn't have to work tomorrow, so it may be a good time to go car shopping."

"I'll pencil it in my schedule. I'm still hunting Nazis but will be home around five or so."

"Nazis? Watch yourself. I think we'll have a bar-b-que for dinner, how's that sound?"

"Sounds good to me. See you later." We smooched through the phone and hung up."

"Do you have to do that kissy face stuff?" Deacon asked.

"Hey, I love my wife. Any chance I can kiss her is good," I replied.

"Well, keep it down around me." He laughed and drove on.

We arrived at the address on the card, a house in a quiet little suburb. It was one of those streets where the builder used one blueprint for all the houses. Every house was the same all down the street.

Deacon knocked on the door and it opened. A very attractive woman of about twenty smiled and said, "May I help you?"

*

Chapter 20

"Yes, Miss, does Louis Reese live here?" Deacon asked.

"He does, or did. He's been missing since last Friday night," she replied, looking a bit upset.

"And you are?" Deacon asked.

"Meredith Reese, Louis' wife," she replied.

"Have you reported him missing to the police?"

"Aren't you the police? I thought you were here to give me some word on his disappearance."

"No, we're here on a different matter. Did you report him being missing?"

"Yes, Saturday afternoon. I went in, and they took my report but said they couldn't look for him yet, that he could have just gone off and didn't bother to mention it to me. They told me if he hadn't come back by Tuesday and I heard no word from him to call them. Today's Tuesday and I was going to go back and report it."

"Miss, can we come in? We have some information about him."

She gave us a blank look then pushed open the screen door. We went in, and she led us to the living room and asked us to sit.

"He's dead, isn't he?" she said quietly.

"I'm sorry, but he was murdered. We're investigating his death. Can you tell me about his association with the Neo-Nazi group?" Deacon asked.

"Those sons-a-bitches, they led him into this." She was tearing up and got a tissue from the coffee table. "I warned him not to get involved, but he wanted to join. He wanted to be part of their group, to show he was tough like they were. Did they do this?"

"No. Does the name Taylor Higgs ring a bell?"

"Higgs, yes, Louis mentioned him as someone who was bothering the group. He did mention that he was going to talk to Higgs last week. Could he be the one who murdered my husband?"

"We're still investigating it, but did your husband go to see Higgs?"

"He didn't tell me if he did. He left here Friday around noon. That's the last I saw of him. Where is his body now?"

Pasta Murders

"It's in the Clark County morgue. You can go in anytime to claim the body. But I want to warn you, his body is not in good shape. It's a little unpleasant looking."

"I'll remember that," she said, tearing up more.

Deacon handed her his business card. "Call me if you need anything or remember anything about your husband and Higgs. We'll let ourselves out. Sorry for your loss."

We stood. She didn't move. We went out the front door and to the car. "I hate telling family that a loved one is dead. I'd rather be a bicycle cop on the strip than deliver news like that."

I remembered Trapper telling us back when he was a bike cop here, he hated it. One of the reasons he moved to Michigan. "So did we learn anything?" I asked.

"We have a timeline as to the body in the tub. We know he was a Nazi, and he went to see Higgs. My money is on Higgs for murdering Reese. He was going to dispose of the body, but didn't finish the job. I'll have to call Joe Lang and give him the ID for his death certificate."

We got in the car and headed back to the precinct. As Deacon parked I said, "If we have nothing else pressing, I think I'll go get Penny and Carol and go car shopping. That way we can work on this all day tomorrow. Has Williams found a storage unit yet?"

"I haven't heard from him. I'll check and see. We can go hunting for storage tomorrow. You can rent one for all that furniture you're going to own."

I smiled at the thought. "Yep, I may have a storage auction with it. I'll talk to you later, unless you figure something out." I got out of the car and went to my van. I sat and called Penny.

"Are you two at home now?" I asked when she answered.

"We are. What's up?"

"I thought we all would go car shopping."

"Oh, goodie, I love shopping." She giggled in the phone.

"I didn't say we were going to the Boulevard Mall. Just to the Vegas Auto Mall. They have the biggest selection."

"I'll tell Carol. See you soon then," she said and hung up.

I drove to the house and found the women on the front lawn with Willy chasing butterflies again. Penny chased and caught Willy, and they came to the van.

I drove them to one of the car dealers on the strip of road that had various dealers selling everything from Audi to Chevy to Volkswagens. That was where I bought my first car when I lived there back in 2003. It was a 1989 Cadillac, the kind that still had character, before they started turning caddies into giant bubbles.

We pulled in, and I could see three salesmen all struggling to get out the office door and over to us. One survived the rush and reached us, smiling like it was Christmas morning.

"Hello, folks, can I put you in a car today?" he said with a fake grin.

Pasta Murders

"You can try, but I'd rather get in myself. You couldn't lift me," I said as a joke, but he looked blank. I guess it went over his head. "We need an economy car for driving to work and shopping. Nothing big, just easy on gas."

"Is this for yourself?" he asked.

"No, for my daughter," I said proudly and indicated her.

"Ah, I see, well let me show you a few vehicles." And he did for the next forty minutes, showing us just about every car on the lot. Carol liked them all, but I managed to find fault with each one.

He suddenly did a double take and looked at Penny. "Say, you're Penny Wickens aren't you?"

"Last time I looked at my driver's license, I was," she said, and that old joke didn't go over his head. He laughed.

"Then that makes you Jim Richards, I presume?" I gave up on the jokes and said I was.

He continued, "Wow, I have to show you the better cars then. I can't have you driving around in these lemons." He led us to another part of the dealership where the cars looked much better. After a few minutes of looking I saw the car for Carol. A 2009 Prius, just like Lynn's car. I had ridden in it enough times to know it was a good car. Carol loved it. Penny smiled.

An hour later, the deal was done, and Carol followed us out of the car lot in her new car. I was wondering where we were going to park all the cars at home. We'd have to get a county permit for a parking lot. I smiled to myself.

We got back and managed to park everyone. I put my van back in its usual spot with the Prius next to it facing the guesthouse.

Penny took Carol around back to the B-B-Q grill that we referred to as the incinerator. It was a huge adobe grill that actually looked like a nuclear reactor. They had been getting ready to cook burgers on the grill when I called, so they had everything ready. I touched a match to the briquettes and a fire ball shot up high enough to knock out a plane. I sometimes get carried away with the starter fluid.

We had our food and were resting by the pool. Willy was swimming with Carol. I was surprised Penny hadn't gone in, but she said she wanted to sit with me and watch the children play. I laughed.

"So how was your day?" she asked.

"Filled with gay Nazi political escorts, and Deacon is a woman in men's clothing."

She looked over at me. "I'm not even going to ask."

"Good, because I wouldn't believe me either." I smiled.

Carol and Willy got out of the pool and sat next to us. "I really want to thank you for all you've done. This has been the best time of my life."

"Quite all right, glad you're happy," I said. "I'll give you a map to Angelo's so you won't get lost. I have an extra GPS to help, too. I'll set it up for you." I looked over and she was tearing up. "Are you all right?"

Pasta Murders

"I'm just overwhelmed by all this. I never had much in my life, now all of a sudden, I have everything, even a family."

I remembered about the DNA swabs but decided to wait. No sense in ruining this moment.

Penny and I were in bed, cuddling, by ten. Willy was on his Bate's Motel chair, the one I bought from the scary motel we stayed at during the magic convention. It was quiet in the house. I had the perimeter alarms set and had warned Carol about wandering in the yard at night. I was wide awake, but Penny was snoozing and snoring softly. I thought about the day and all that was going on. Horn was dead, Higgs was dead, one Nazi was dead. No victim to vindicate. Turns out they all were not nice people.

I'd call Angelo in the morning to tell him I was sending his poster of the review with Carol. I managed to get it done in the middle of driving here and there. That would make him happy. Penny rolled over on her side, and I got up and went to the kitchen. I felt a presence behind me and jumped to find Willy at my heels.

"Thanks, dog, I almost wet my pants. Would you like a late night snack, too?" Willy sat, wagging his tiny tail. "Okay, give me a minute." I pulled out his kibble and poured a bowl for him. He munched as I got out the bagels and cream cheese from the fridge. I jumped again when I heard a voice.

"And you weren't going to invite me for bagels and cream cheese?" Penny said, standing in the doorway.

Chapter 21

Penny sat at the snack bar waiting for me to serve her the bagel. After toasting it, I lathered it up with a generous dollop of cream cheese. She bounced on her stool as I placed it in front of her. "I love your bagels and cream cheese," she said with a smile as she took a big bite. She smiled at me with cream cheese on her upper lip. I came over and licked it from her lip. She giggled.

We finished and went back to bed where we cuddled some more until we both were sound asleep. The next morning she was out the door on her way to work. I had called Lacey to pick up Willy as I wanted to get an early start with Deacon. I went out to give Angelo's poster to Carol to take to him and to set up the GPS for her to help her find her way around Vegas. She thanked me and drove off.

I felt nervous as I watched Carol driving away, her first time out in the car in this crazy city. I hoped she would be all right. I saw Lacey coming up the road. Willy was standing next to me, and he must have seen her, also. He ran over to her and jumped up and down as she parked in the drive. She got out and bent down to pick him up.

"Thanks, Lacey, I'll try to stop in later."

"You better, and you need to sit down with me so I can tell you about my vacation."

I cringed.

"I saw that. Now I'll bring in photos to show you, too. I took hundreds," she said with a laugh, then got back in her car with Willy and drove off.

Lacey could drive me crazy, but she was a good person. I went to my Crown Vic and pulled it out of the garage to drive today to let the van rest. I drove to the precinct and parked. Deacon was in Lynn's office, and I sat waiting while he was on the phone. He nodded to me.

He finished his call and said, "Good morning, ready to start?"

"Sure, what's your plan?"

"Williams came up with one storage unit that was listed in Horn's name. It's out on Industrial Drive, over by your office."

"Okay, I've seen that place. I forgot it was out there."

"So shall we go?" Deacon asked as he stood. I got up and followed him to the motor pool to get the Charger again.

We drove over and went by my office on the way. There were a couple cars in the parking lot, and I wondered what they wanted. Trapper and Earl could handle it. Unless it was for Buck and his guards. I'd find out later.

We arrived at the storage units and parked by the office. We went in and Deacon showed his badge to the young person behind the counter.

"I need to talk to a Mike," Deacon said.

"I'm Mike. Is this about the call I got yesterday?"

"If it involves Alfred Horn and his storage unit, yes. Can you direct us there?"

"Sure, do you have a warrant?"

Deacon leaned across the counter. "Listen, junior, Horn is dead and I'm investigating his death. You wouldn't know anything about it, would you?"

The young man looked surprised then said, "I don't know anything."

"Maybe I should take you in and question you."

He was getting nervous now.

"Do I smell weed on you?" Deacon was spreading it thick.

The young man quickly said, "I'll take you to the unit. I don't have a key so you'll have to break in."

He headed to the door as we followed. Down a row and over one, we came to a unit that was no longer locked. The lock was cut.

"Wow, I didn't know about this," the kid said.

"Go back to your office and get the security tapes for this area ready for me to take with me when I leave," Deacon said. Mike nodded and ran off.

"I have a feeling there won't be much in here," I said, thinking back to the Dominatrix murders when I was in the same situation. A storage unit had been broken into and evidence removed.

Deacon pulled up the door and started to go in. I was behind him when I felt something whiz past my head. The bullet hit the metal side of the unit and made a loud noise. I darted to the inside of the unit and pushed up against the side wall. Deacon had his gun out and was standing next to me.

"Someone doesn't want us in here," he said. He tried to look around the opening but was greeted with

Pasta Murders

another shot. He ducked back in, took out his cell phone and called for back-up.

We waited it out as we heard sirens coming up the road. The shooter was no doubt gone by that time. Deacon peeked around the opening again. No more shots. He said he couldn't see anything. The patrol cars came flying into the drive and stopped as Deacon came out of the unit. He gave an explanation, and the patrol officers went to the area where the shooter could have been hiding judging from the direction of the shots.

"Okay, we're getting close. Someone wanted to warn us not to snoop in here," Deacon said.

"So shall we snoop?" I asked.

He smiled, and we entered the unit. It was a small unit, and there was very little inside. A couple of boxes and a file cabinet.

"Did someone already take evidence out of here? Did they cut the lock today or yesterday? Or did we interrupt them?" I asked.

Deacon opened the file cabinet and pulled out files. "These are old. Some have dates on them from the sixties. There seem to be a few missing, judging by the empty file folders. Someone did get a few before we got here." He looked at the tabs. "The names on some of these files are from the offices of the Senate Committee on un-American activities. But they're now empty."

"McCarthyism era commie files. Someone didn't want that info released. In 1950 Joseph McCarthy, a senator from Wisconsin, claimed to have a list of 205 people in the State Department that were possible

140

commie sympathizers. It was a black period in our history. Lots of people lost important jobs because of McCarthy witch hunts."

"Could this be the info that got Horn and Higgs murdered?" Deacon asked.

"I'm sure it was, but how do we interrogate politicians from over fifty years ago, and what do they have in common with this?"

A patrol officer came in and said, "Detective, we couldn't find anyone. We did find some shell casings. I bagged them and will turn them over to CSI when they get here."

"Good work. See if you can get the security tapes from the kid in the office. Have CSI check them to see who may have broken in here."

The officer said he would and went out. Deacon continued, "This all has to be carefully guarded. The government may swoop in to take them away, and we'll never know what happened. I'll call Warren and have him box up everything in the file cabinet and hide it in the evidence locker." He went to the side of the unit and called Warren.

CSI rolled in but Deacon held them off until Warren and Williams arrived and started to pack the files. The CSI supervisor protested the taking of evidence. Deacon explained it was a matter of national security.

"I can call Harold and get his take on this," I said.

"Do you trust him?" Deacon asked me.

"With my life. He's always been there when I needed him."

141

"Okay, call him but don't say where the files are."

"I'll call later. Let's help pack up all this stuff and get it safely out."

Warren and Williams took the boxes we got from the storage office, now packed, and put them in Warren's car. I was standing in the drive between the units, looking around, when Deacon came up and asked, "What's up?"

"I have the feeling we're being watched. Maybe they haven't left."

Deacon looked around the area and saw nothing. "Nah, they scooted out when the cavalry arrived. Let's go in and dig through the files. We may discover something yet."

I agreed, and we drove back to the precinct. Deacon called Warren and said to get a dolly and take the files to Lynn's office, but to do it discreetly.

Deacon parked, and we went in. The three boxes of files had been put in the corner of the room.

We went to them and dug into the first box. Deacon called Warren in and gave him a pile of files to examine. The three of us sat in the office going through the papers. After a couple hours we were getting nowhere, and we had just about finished with all the files.

"I see nothing criminal in these. I saw a bit of impropriety in some departments of the government but no dirty secrets that would be a reason for murder. Probably the good files were removed," Deacon said, standing to stretch.

I dropped the files I had and stood, also, then walked out of the office. "Want something to drink? I need a Pepsi."

"Yeah, let's take a break. Greg, come on and I'll buy." The three of us went to the breakroom and got our drinks from the machines. We sat for a while, relaxing, then finished our sodas and went back to the office. We were surprised to see a number of black suited men carrying the boxes out of Deacon's office.

Deacon stormed over and said, "What the hell are you doing? Stop this!"

One man who looked like he was in charge said, "Detective DeAngelo, stand down or you will be arrested for interference." He held out a badge of the Secret Service.

*

Chapter 22

I figured Deacon knew he couldn't fight them, so he tried to be friendly. "Okay, listen, you wouldn't have these files if we hadn't found them, so why not give us a little cooperation so I can close my murder case?"

The agent stood silently for a moment, then said, "We've had Horn under surveillance for a while. We knew he had files of a delicate nature, but we had no idea where. We also had your people under surveillance after Horn turned up dead. We followed your activities, and now we have the files back. Our government thanks you." He spun on his heels and went out of the squad room.

"If that don't beat all," Deacon muttered. "They were watching us? I wonder if they had our conversations bugged, too?"

"At least we managed to get through all the files before they took them," I said.

"But we didn't find anything connecting to Horn or Higgs," Warren said.

"There wouldn't be. Horn just had the damaging info that someone wanted. Now the files are back with the government, and they can relax," Deacon offered.

"But they aren't back, at least not all of them. There were files missing, and we don't know what they were. I'm sure the government will not be happy to see that they came up short," I said.

"Whatever. I think we need to go back to the beginning and start with Horn's murder. Why was he killed in Angelo's restaurant? What's the connection there?" Deacon asked.

"Someone wanted to get him out of his apartment? They lured him there and trashed his place, while they interrogated him about his safeguard." I looked at my watch and said, "I need to get a storage unit and get the furnishings moved out of the towers. I'll check back with you later. For now we're at a standstill."

"Okay, I'll call if anything breaks," Deacon said and went back into the office. I went out to my Crown Vic and drove back to the storage place. Mike was still there. I got two big units and paid him for three months.

"Do you know any movers who can pack and move a couple apartments?" I asked Mike.

He pulled a card from his desk and handed it to me. "These guys are good. We've used them before."

I put the card in my jacket pocket and thanked him. I went back to my car and drove down the road to my office. I wanted to call Harold.

I parked and went in, saying hello to Tracey in her little domain up front, then on to find Lacey talking to Earl.

"Well, I see you're not in federal custody," he said with a grin.

"Okay, I give."

"We had a visit from the Secret Service. They were asking questions about you. Lacey lied through her teeth, and I think they bought it," Earl said.

Lacey smacked his arm and said, "I did not lie. I told them the truth. Jim is really a dangerous spy and was hiding out here."

"Fun's fun. Now what happened?" I asked with a frown.

"They were asking if we knew where you were," Lacey said. "They wanted to talk to you. We told them you were probably with Deacon. Then they left. That was all."

"I don't need to be watched by the Feds. I'm going to call Harold and see if he can get to the bottom of this. Oh, and he said you still owe him that rum."

Pasta Murders

Earl laughed and said, "Tell him it will be delivered."

I went to my office followed by Willy who came out of somewhere. I picked him up and put him on my desk then reached for my desk phone. With my hand on the receiver, I stopped, thinking that the Feds could have it bugged. I stood and went to my door yelling for Earl.

He came in from the lobby and said, "You bellowed?"

"Do you have any toys that can tell if my phones are being tapped?"

"Think the Feds are still after you?" he said with a grin. "I'll go get my toy." He went back to his office as I looked at Willy who stood on my desk wagging his tail.

A few moments later Earl came in with a small black box that had lights and buttons on it. He scanned the phone and the wiring and smiled. "You're clean. No one listening."

"Go check the rest of the building for bugs or whatever. Do a complete sweep."

"I'll have to get out my super-duper-spy detector. I haven't used it in a very long while." He went out. I sat, found Harold's number and dialed.

About six rings later, Harold answered. "You know I'll have to change my private number if you and Earl keep calling." He laughed.

"Then how would you know when Earl is sending the rum?" I replied. "I have a mystery. Maybe you can pull something out for me?"

"I'll try, but you know it will cost."

"What? You're already getting a case of rum. You don't ask for much do you?"

"Hey, I work for the government. I have to get all the perks I can in order to survive," he said with a bigger laugh. "What do you want now? I know you had a run-in with Secret Service already? What more do you need?"

"That happened just over an hour ago. How could you know already?"

"Those classified files that were found are news all through the grapevine. Our country owes you a debt of gratitude for protecting the guilty from being exposed. Now do you want to hear what I found after our last conversation?"

"I'm waiting on pins and needles," I said sarcastically.

"Word is from some of my sources that those files contained info on a very respectable Senator who's running for the high office of President. Files that were lost years ago after an investigation into charges that this Senator may have connections to the Nazi movement."

I felt like putting my head on my desk and bashing my brains out with the phone. This mess was not going to go away. "So this Senator would do anything to get the files back. Why is this just coming out now? Why didn't they get closure on him years ago?"

"The man is powerful, and he went to great lengths to see that all the original files were destroyed. But—the big but—it turns out Horn had taken the files before they were supposedly destroyed in a mysterious fire. It didn't come to light back then. This guy thought he was clean. Since the good honest Senator is now running for office, his forces are doing all they can to be sure to bury his past."

"Where are you getting all this information?" I asked. My head was starting to ache.

"Jim, I'm hurt that you don't know what I do. To you, I may be a simple FBI agent, but that's only my cover. I have connections to the NSA, CIA, FBI and every other letter you can think of. All intel goes through my office, and I disseminate and analyze it to be sure nothing tips the balance of power in the government."

"So you're an ombudsman?"

"Well, that's a simplification, but yes. I monitor all activities and make sure we live in a safer world."

"You must make men quake in their shoes," I said with a smile.

"Oh, I do, my friend. Now you have no problems with the files. They have been salvaged by the Feds."

"Well, not exactly. Some files were missing. Probably the Senator's misconduct files."

"Then it probably was the Senator's people. No one else would have bothered to go to the trouble to take them away."

"Except the opposing side in the race for President."

"True, our standing President would love to have ammunition against Macey."

"Macey? Is he the Senator? I never liked him. I didn't know he was going to run," I said, surprised.

"He just announced it today, as a matter of fact. Probably figured the files had been recovered by his people, and he was safe."

"So Horn and Higgs died trying to protect our country from its first Nazi President."

"And we will never prove anything. No one knows he engineered all this."

"But you do. What's protecting you?"

"I admit to nothing. And I'm really Batman." He laughed. "Now you just need to find Horn's killer. I'm sure it wasn't Macey's people. They don't operate that way, too much scandal if they're caught. Good luck. I have to go back to saving the U.S. from its own government." He hung up.

I sat back in my chair with a new respect for Harold. He'd been an oddball in the past, but I never knew his influence over things. Earl came back into my office and said he found nothing covert other than our own security cameras and microphones.

He left, and I thought about calling Deacon with this new info, but decided to wait. I pulled out the business card for the movers and called. I made arrangements for them to clean out the two apartments and store everything in the two storage units. I got the biggest ones they had to be sure everything would fit. It would take time to go through everything, throwing out junk, saving good stuff and selling off things like the fertility statues. Then, hopefully, there would be enough good furniture to get Carol started in her own place.

My cell phone buzzed. The Caller ID said it was Deacon. "I was just going to call you. What's up?"

"I got a call from someone identifying himself as an agent of the Secret Service wanting to know where the rest of the files were. I told him that was all we got and explained about the storage unit being broken into. I'm sure he wasn't happy about that."

*

Chapter 23

I passed on all the info that Harold told me except the part about what exactly Harold does. Deacon listened intently and then sighed loudly when I finished.

"I'm sure this is going to be a big deal government interference project now. We'll have Feds roaming the halls here looking for classified documents that we don't have. I wouldn't have taken Macey for the Nazi type. He seems to me to be a tight ass right wing Conservative."

"Well, left wing liberals aren't ones to be Nazis, either," I said. "If those missing files are in the hands of Macey's people then this all means nothing. They'll destroy them and that will be it. Now if the opposing team has them, it could be a different ballgame. Then Macey is done for."

"Politics are not my worry. I just want to find the murderer of Horn and Higgs. I think the evil ones in government did it, but we can't prove it or get a conviction. Any ideas?"

"You're the lead detective on this, you tell me," I said trying not to laugh.

"Well, I was thinking about bringing in the Nazi guy who identified Reese. He may shed some light on this."

"I never did catch his name."

"Arnold Liebman. I'm going to have a car go pick him up as a material witness in the death of Reese. Come on in if you want to watch or help."

"I'll be right over," I said and hung up.

I went through the lobby again. Lacey was at her desk with Willy sleeping on the corner.

"I have to go interrogate a Nazi. Be back later."

She looked at me and said, "Sure, any lame excuse to get out of the office. You better come back."

"I will," I said and went out to my car.

I drove back to the precinct and went in to see Deacon sitting in the squad room. "Whatcha doing out here?"

He pointed to Lynn's office where Weber and some guy looking like a Fed were sitting behind closed doors.

"What the hell are they doing here?" I asked.

"The Secret Service came storming in and wants the files of our investigation of Horn's death," he said, sounding dejected.

"They want the missing files or your files on Horn's case?" I asked.

"They want Horn's case files. They think it may help them to find the missing confidential files. I told Weber we didn't have them and didn't know where they are. Right now they can take the whole damn case. I'm fed up with all this."

"Do you have the head Nazi in for questioning?"

"Yep, and I didn't say anything to Weber or the governmental monkey in there about him. If I do, I figure the Feds will take him away, and we'll never know what went on with Reese."

"Did you put the info in your case file about Reese?"

"I was going to, but hadn't got around to it yet."

"Good. We have an edge then. Let's wait until the Feds leave, and then we can question Liebman."

"That's what I've been waiting for," Deacon said with a smile.

The door to Lynn's office opened, and Weber came out followed by the agent. "Detective DeAngelo, turn over what you have on the Horn case." Then he went back down the hallway to his office.

Deacon stood, tossed the murder book at the agent and said, "Have fun, asshole. If you solve the case let us know."

The man tried to hold onto the pages that were falling out of the book. He had to stoop to the floor to gather up the ones he couldn't hold. When he finally had all of them together, he stood, glared at Deacon and left.

"You do have a copy, right?" I asked.

"Nope." Deacon grinned. "I gave him the photocopied pages. I have the originals. It's LVMPD property even if he is a Fed. Screw him. Shall we go talk to our Nazi?"

"Make sure the Fed is out of the building," I said.

He smiled at me and asked Warren to go see if the man had left the building. We waited until Warren came back with thumbs up. We went to interrogation and found Leibman pacing the room. We entered.

"What the hell kind of treatment is this?" he roared.

"Sorry, we were busy. There was an agent of the Secret Service here asking about you," Deacon lied.

His eyes went wide, and he sat. "Why were they interested in me," he said, suddenly much quieter.

"Gee, maybe you can tell us," Deacon said. "Have you done something to piss off the Feds?"

"Not that I know. Why am I here?" he asked.

"All we want is a little info. Maybe you can help us, and we can help you."

"How can you help me?"

"Put in a good word with the Feds for you."

"You'd do that?" he asked, the panic in his eyes ebbing a little.

"Sure. Now answer my questions."

"Anything," he said and sat back looking relieved.

"Tell me everything you know about Albert Horn and Taylor Higgs."

Liebman went blank, staring at the mirror across from him. "I don't know anything about Reese's death."

"I didn't ask you about Reese. I asked you what you knew about Horn and Higgs."

Pasta Murders

"Higgs was a pain in the ass. He took it to be his calling to harass us for what we stand for. He made phone calls to our friends and employers telling them we were Nazis and we wanted to eradicate everyone except white people. He didn't let up."

"So you killed him?"

"What? No, I didn't do that. Reese said he was going to have a talk with Higgs. I didn't stop him, but I had no idea he was going to kill Higgs."

"He didn't kill Higgs. Reese was dead days before Higgs died. Maybe your people found out and retaliated."

"Hell, I was the only one who knew he went to visit Higgs," he said, then shut up as the realization hit him that he might be implicating himself. "I need a lawyer."

"Look, Liebman, all we want is some info about the men. We aren't looking at you for murder…yet."

"I knew nothing about Horn. He was just some food reviewer. Higgs was his friend from what I hear. They were a little too close, if you know what I mean."

"They were gay, we got that. Did that bother your people?"

"It bothered me. I can't speak for everyone else. Look, I don't know anything about the killing of Horn, Higgs or even Reese. That's all I'm saying without a lawyer."

Deacon shot a glance at me. I shrugged. "Okay, get out of here. But we may need to talk to you again so stick around."

Liebman got up quickly and left the room. A uniform escorted him to the exit. Deacon sat back and sighed loudly. He was doing that a lot lately.

"Still nowhere are we," I said.

"Yep, I'm going to go home for lunch and see how my baby wife is doing. She wasn't happy to be restricted to bed."

"I should go back to the office and let Lacey finally tell me about her and Mac's vacation before she has a fit. I like Lacey, she's sarcastically funny. She has a quick wit and makes the office run smoothly. I'd hate to lose her."

"Okay, if anything pops, I'll call." He stood, and we went out of interrogation. We both left the building, Deacon to his Prius and me to my Crown Vic. I wondered how Carol was doing with her new Prius. I hoped I didn't get a call from the police or a hospital.

I realized it was different having a son as opposed to a daughter. My son was a good kid and rarely got into any trouble. I was proud of him and the way he turned out. However, a daughter, as I was finding out, was cause for worry. They had to be nurtured and cared for, although I was about thirty years late for that with Carol. She was a grown woman and had been fending for herself for years. Her mother wasn't the brightest bulb, and I felt sure Carol often had to take care of her. Oh, well, I'd do the best I could. Then I remembered the swabs I still had. It needed to be done, to ease our minds.

I arrived at the office to find Penny and Carol's cars parked out front. Oh, great. The women were going to gang up on me. I hoped Earl or Trapper was in. I went through the outer lobby, saying hi to Tracey as I passed. Poor girl, out there all alone. As I came through the glass doors to the main lobby I heard laughter. I hoped that was a good sign. Then again maybe they were laughing about me. I always had a guilty conscience.

"Well, the prodigal son returns," Lacey said with a smile. Penny was at the counter with Carol and came to me with a big kiss.

"Catch your killer yet?" she asked.

"Nope, and I'm not sure we ever will. The government is making waves, and we may drown in their wake."

"Government? What do they have to do with it?" she asked.

"I'll explain it all later. Now can I hear about this great vacation of Lacey and Mac?" I said to get it over with. Not that I didn't care, I just had things on my mind about the case.

Lacey stood and brought a huge photo album to the counter. I would have cringed, but she probably would have hit me with the book. So I smiled and waited.

Everyone gathered close, looking at the pictures as Lacey explained every aspect of the trip to the Grand Canyon. I was ready to view hundreds of pictures of rocks and valleys.

*

Chapter 24

An hour and a half later, Lacey finished her tour. Earl made the mistake of coming out around page 10 of the 200 page photo album to see what we were doing. He was trapped. I had to admit the photos were good and not just of rocks and valleys. Lacey had a good eye for photography.

Penny latched on to me and said, "We need to get some food. Take us to an expensive restaurant."

I looked at Carol still standing at the counter with Lacey going over a few more photos. Earl had managed to slip out earlier with an excuse.

"Don't you think we'd offend Angelo if we went to another restaurant?" I said.

"True, and Angelo's is not cheap, so Momma Mia would be a good place to go. Shall I tell Carol?"

I knew enough not to argue with Penny. "Sure, go ahead." Penny went over to the girls gabbing about the photos, and I suddenly remembered the swabs. Might as well do it now. I waited until they finished and Penny came to me with Carol.

"Before we go there's one matter that needs to be taken care of. Let's go into my office." I led them through the inner glass doors, down the hall and into my office. I heard a noise and saw Willy coming through his doggie door to follow us.

I went around the back of my desk were I had put the swabs in the drawer. Penny and Carol stood in the front, Willy at my feet. I scooped him up and placed him on the desk.

I put the two vials on the desk and said to Carol, "You still want to do this?"

She looked a little sad, but said firmly, "Yes. We should, just to ease both our minds."

Following the directions Deacon had given me, I took one vial, went around to Carol and popped the top then took out the stick with a cotton tip on it. "Open up," I said. She did. I wiped the tip around in her mouth, picking up saliva. I put the swab back in the vial and wrote her name on it. I repeated the process on myself using the second vial, wrote my name on it and put both of them in another bag then sealed it.

"We've committed to this now, so what will happen, happens." I, too, was feeling a little sad about this, but kept it to myself. I really wanted Carol to be my daughter, but I had to know the truth.

She didn't look much better than the way I felt, but smiled and said, "We need to know."

"Okay, I'll give these to Deacon, and he'll turn them over to the right people for testing. Now shall we get some food?"

We left, and I drove everyone over to Angelo's. Penny called Angelo to warn him we were coming. He greeted us at the door.

"Ah, my favorite people." He grinned as he took us to a table. I looked over to the table where Horn expired. It was gone. "Did you remove the death table?" I asked.

"Ah, yeah, it was a bit morbid to have it out here. If people want to see it, I put it out back in the alley." He laughed. "Now I have a special meal planned for you. I'll have Lonnie come take your drink orders." He went off, and Lonnie came up and wrote down our drink requests.

Carol was grinning. "Angelo told me he might train me in the kitchen. I'd love that. I've always loved cooking."

"Well, listen and learn. Angelo is a fantastic cook, or I should say, chef."

We sat talking about Carol's trip around Vegas in her new car. She had a few problems getting lost, but got to know where some important places were, like the Mall and the strip. She loved driving up the strip in the sunshine and dry air. She said she was amazed by all the people wandering around.

"I couldn't believe they allowed people to walk around with drinks in their hands," she said.

"It's a very liberal town. They even put up with the men who hand out flyers for escort services, but only in certain areas. They can get annoying when you're walking up and down the strip," I said.

Our food came, and we enjoyed the delicious feast. Angelo knew how to please his guests. I kept looking over to the empty spot where the missing table had been. I had seen the body with his head in the plate of pasta. It was not a pleasant sight. It was good that Angelo took the table out.

We finished, and Angelo brought over a bottle of brandy and four glasses. He poured the amber liquid and made a toast to us.

159

Pasta Murders

"Two years ago I came here to watch my mother marry Gino. My mother was kidnapped, and Jim brought her back. I thank you, my friend. I really feel like you are my family here in Vegas, and that makes me feel very good."

"Thank you, Angelo. You are a good friend and a part of our family which seems to be growing." I looked at Carol.

She blushed and smiled.

"Now shall we go catch a show on the strip?" I asked. I had already called ahead and set up tickets for the Blue Man Group.

"Where do you suggest?" Penny asked.

"Just follow my lead. Angelo, I got extra tickets for you to come, too."

He gave me a big grin and said, "I'll go tell my manager, Harvey Rush, that I'm taking the night off. Wait for me."

He left and came back about twenty minutes later. He had changed his clothes and looked very dapper in his black suit, black shirt and black tie. I thought of him as a very well-dressed gangster, but kept it to myself. He looked good.

Harvey Rush came up and asked where we were headed. "It's going to be a surprise," I replied.

"Have you caught Horn's killer yet?" he asked.

"We have many leads, but not close enough. It's an ongoing case. Hopefully we'll have something soon."

"I hope you close your case," he said and went off.

I put down a nice tip for Lonnie. I knew she could get through college on the tips my friends and I gave her. I smiled at the thought. I paid at the register by the door, took a mint from the glass bowl, and we headed out. I had brought Penny's car which had more room than mine, hoping Angelo would come with us.

We arrived at the Venetian, and I pulled into valet parking. I didn't feel like roaming the parking structure, navigating the elevators and ultimately finding my way to the show room. We were seated by the time the show started. It was as good as the first time I saw the Blue Man Group when they were in the Luxor years ago when I lived there the first time.

The show ended, and the three of us went out to the lobby where the band was lined up to greet the audience. We shook their hands, complimenting them on the show, returned to valet parking, and they brought out our car.

Back at the restaurant, Angelo invited us in for late night drinks. We had to turn him down. Penny, Carol and I all had to work the next morning. Angelo thanked us for the nice evening and went back into his restaurant. I drove up the strip before returning home. I didn't have the opportunity to see the strip at night with all the lights lit that often, so I took advantage.

We got back home and Willy let us know he was not happy to be left alone. After reassuring Willy she still loved him, Carol went to the guesthouse. Penny and I went into the bedroom and undressed to crawl under the sheets. It was too late for TV and we were both tired, so we let Willy sleep with us and cuddled.

The next morning, I got a call from the moving people. They were at the apartments and wanted to know if everything went. I said it did, and they hung up. I was going to go by the storage units later to see if they had packed everything good enough.

"Good morning, Sweetie," Penny said as she came into the kitchen where I was making my toast. "I'll take Willy today. He needs some time with me. I don't see him as much as you do."

I didn't want to admit that Willy spent more time with Lacey than with me. "Who's on your show today?" I asked to change the subject.

"Honestly, I don't know. Gordy has been changing things on me, so I'm often surprised when I get there."

"Doesn't give you much time to find out more about your guests."

"I'm a quick reader. The bios they give me help. Most of the questions are written down before I get there. The thing is so canned, I could be home calling in my hosting," she said, sounding a little down.

"Are you getting tired of this?"

"No, I love what I'm doing and all the celebrities I meet. It's fun but just a little…well, dull."

"How could you spice it up?" I asked.

She smiled. "I have some ideas, like going out on the strip and talking to tourists, going into the casinos and talking to gamblers. The heart and breath of Vegas, the gamblers and tourists. They are as important as celebrities. We need more contact with people. The show is getting stale."

"Well, tell Gordy you want to do that, and if he refuses, quit."

"I just may. Then I'll come into your office and become a private investigator." She smiled and went to the bedroom.

When she was out of sight, I cringed.

*

Chapter 25

I had the DNA test vials in my pocket as I entered LVMPD precinct to see Deacon. I had no idea about where to investigate next. Maybe Deacon had come up with something.

"Good morning," I said as I entered Lynn's office. Deacon was seated at the desk looking at some papers. He put them down and sat back. I set the envelope of the vials in front of him. He put it in his desk drawer and thanked me. Then he continued.

"I had Warren run Higgs' background and came up with some interesting things. It seems Higgs was involved in gay prostitution for hire back in New York and it came out he tried to blackmail a number of clients. Some big hitters in the Big Apple. He scooted on the charges, seemed he still had names and dates of his clients and they decided it was better if he just left New York. Higgs went to Detroit, but it wasn't very friendly towards him so he moved to

Vegas. He met Horn through mutual friends, and they got together."

"Well, that's enlightening. What was the reaction of the men…boys that Higgs had working for him here when they were brought in?"

"They were all over eighteen, just young looking. They clammed up, but admitted they were hired to take appointments for clients. Simple bust for Vice. Still doesn't help find the killer."

"Higgs must have stored up money from prior blackmails. If he knew about Horn's hidden files, maybe he got hold of the files and was doing a little blackmail with them without Horn knowing. Then the people who were being blackmailed decided to get the files back and tortured Horn into giving up the location of the files," I said, sitting at the desk.

"It's a good theory. One that holds up to Higgs' background in blackmail. But we still need to know who was being blackmailed."

"I hear that Macey's in town to stump for his bid as President. Could we go pay him a visit to see what he thinks?" I asked.

"Interesting that he's in town just as Horn and Higgs are murdered. Maybe he wanted to be sure the job was handled properly."

"And visit with some of his Nazi buddies," I said with a smile.

"I don't think he'd go that far. He's running for the leader of the U.S., and he has to be very careful now what with all the damn investigative journalists running around. But I think it wouldn't hurt to go pay him a visit. I'll call the police media office. They'll know where to find him, especially if he needs police protection." Deacon made a phone call, and five minutes later he had a location. He stood. "Let's go shake some trees and see what falls out."

We went to the Wynn Towers and into the lobby. Deacon showed his badge and asked for George Macey's room.

"I'm sorry, sir, but even though you're an officer of the law, I can't give out that information," the girl behind the counter said.

"I figured that much. Now can you call up and get one of his security detail to hurry their butts down here and take us up?"

I liked it when Deacon took on the tough cop routine. The girl looked at her computer and then dialed a number. She spoke quietly, so we couldn't hear, then hung up.

"Someone will be with you shortly," she said and went off.

We wandered around the huge lobby. I said, "This place is another expensive hotel for the rich and mighty. I remember watching it being built when I lived in Vegas before."

In about five minutes an elevator opened, and out came a man. He smiled as he approached us. "They'll let anyone in here, won't they DeAngelo?"

"If you're guarding the candidate, I feel sorry for him, Baker," Deacon replied as they shook hands. Deacon turned to me and said, "Jim, this is Joel Baker, used to be one of LVPD's worst cops. He had to take a private security job. No one else would have him."

"Screw you, Deacon. I'm surprised you're still with it. Now why are you here?"

"We need to speak to Macey about a sensitive matter."

"How sensitive?"

"Could mean his candidacy."

"I don't like where this could be going. Can you fill me in?"

"I really think we should check with the Senator first before letting anyone else know."

"Okay, fair enough, follow me." He led us to the elevator, and we headed up. I left my stomach around the fourth floor. This one was even a little faster than in the towers.

We arrived on the tenth floor and came out to find six men all standing around in the hallway looking like FBI, but it turns out they were private, working for Baker.

Baker took us to a door and knocked. After a few moments it opened, and another man asked what Baker needed.

"Just a moment of the Senator's time to talk to a couple officers of the Las Vegas police," he said casually. I didn't correct him about my presence there.

The man went back into the room and returned a few minutes later, waving us in. The suite was huge and opulent, fitting a wealthy Senator and his people. Personally, I felt he should be more of a man of the people and take a room at one of the motels off the airport. I smiled to myself at the image of that.

"Baker, what's up?" the Senator asked as he lounged in an easy chair wearing a robe. It was partially open, and he wasn't hiding much.

"Sir, this is an old acquaintance of mine from my days on the LVPD. He's with Metro homicide and wants to talk to you."

The Senator stood and walked over to us. "What's this about?" he asked me.

"I'm not a police officer, I'm a civilian consultant. He's the one you need to talk to," I said, pointing to Deacon.

Macey turned to Deacon who said, "I'm Detective DeAngelo, and I need to talk to you privately."

"Privately. Sounds ominous. What could you want with me that would need to be private?"

"Regarding Taylor Higgs or Albert Horn," Deacon said quietly to the man.

He went a couple shades paler, turned and ordered everyone out of the room. They slowly moved out as he picked up a glass I presumed contained alcohol. He waited until everyone cleared the room then turned back to us.

"What about Higgs and Horn? What are they saying about me?" He looked nervous now, starting to sweat in the air conditioned room. Not a good thing for a politician to do.

"They aren't saying much, they're both dead," Deacon replied.

The man looked shocked and moved a few feet away. "I knew nothing about their murders. Was this recent?"

"Within the last three days. There's a lot going on in this case, and we were hoping you could clear up a few facts for us."

"I don't know much other than Horn stole government documents years ago, and Higgs had this idea that he could blackmail me with some dirty details he had."

"What would be so important in those papers that he could even suggest blackmail?" Deacon asked.

Macey went silent. He polished off his drink, then poured another. He took another sip. "How much of what I tell you is going to turn up in some police report?"

"I have to report anything regarding murder. If it's not pertinent to our investigation, I can gloss over it, but I have to report it."

"Higgs was trying to blackmail me about an indiscretion I had years ago."

There was Deacon's word of the day, indiscretion.

"What sort of an indiscretion?"

He was quiet again. "My wife knows, so I guess it's not a big deal. Hell, Clinton came out smelling like a rose even after his dalliance with that woman." He took another sip of his drink.

"Are you saying that Higgs was attempting to blackmail you about a woman you had an affair with?"

"That's what he said, and he had the evidence to back it up. Photos, phone taps, the whole nine yards. I confessed to my wife, but she wants to be First Lady even more than I want to be President. She said she'd overlook it, but if I ever did it again, she's castrate me. You don't mess with a Texas vixen."

Deacon looked at me. I'm sure I looked as puzzled as I felt. He turned back to Macey. "Higgs wasn't trying to blackmail you about your association with the American Nazi Party?"

Macey was so shocked, he almost dropped his drink.

"Where did you hear that?" he demanded.

"Sources. It came to light in my investigation of Horn and his missing files. Someone got into the original files, and some of them are missing. The Feds have the rest of what we found."

Macey went completely white. "You found the original missing documents they said Horn took?"

"We did, but some of the files were missing. The Feds are still looking for them."

"Did you see these files?"

"My associates and I went through them, yes."

"Was there anything about me?" His hand was shaking slightly. I could see the ripples in the drink.

"Didn't see anything related to you. If there were any documents about you, they're in the files that are missing."

Macey turned away from us. "You have no idea who has these files?"

"If we did, we wouldn't be asking you these questions. Can you tell us what was in the files that has you so nervous?"

"I'm not at liberty to say," he said and downed his drink.

*

Chapter 26

"Senator Macey, you may be a big name politician and a candidate for President, but you're still a citizen of the United States and subject to its laws, ones that you may have written. If you aren't going to cooperate, then I may have to take you in for questioning. Let the press see me giving you your Miranda rights. Do you think your public would like that?"

The Senator stared at Deacon for far too long. I hoped Deacon was right about being able to haul Macey's ass in for questioning.

"Detective, I have lived a clean life and I'm running a clean campaign, and I'm not going to have it besmirched now by you."

"Well, I have a job to uphold as a law officer. I will do my job even if it discomforts you."

They were now head to head. I wondered who would blink first.

Macey pulled back and went to pour another drink. "I was stupid and trying to impress a woman. I didn't realize it was the Nazi party until I got there. The woman was crazy, and I distanced myself from her as quickly as I could. But that one night I was seen by certain people, and that was all it took for them to try to ruin my reputation. I was running for Mayor of Arlington, Virginia, at the time. It was the headquarters of the American Nazi Party. I wanted them out of the city, but having been seen in the company of them made it bad for my campaign. I lost the election, but went on to run for governor. I won that one. Two years later, I ran for the Senate and won that, also. I was told that the files that contained that awful incident were buried. Until Higgs showed up and started his crap about it." He took a big sip of the drink.

"Was that enough for you to murder him?" Deacon threw out.

Macey straightened and met Deacon's gaze. "I can survive being seen in the company of Nazis, but murder is not something I can hide. No, I had nothing to do with his death. Or Horn's. Detective, do you have any further questions?"

"Aren't you worried about who has the files now?" he asked.

The Senator paused and thought about it. "I have no idea, but I'm sure if my enemies have them, it will come to light, and you can question them about the murder."

Deacon said, "I hope for your sake we catch them before they ruin your spotless reputation."

Deacon nodded to me, and we left the room. He waved to Baker, and we went to the elevator. We were inside with the doors sliding shut when a hand appeared between them. Baker.

He pulled the door open enough to get on then let it close. The elevator began its descent as Baker stood facing Deacon.

"I'm not sure what you said to the Senator, but he is a good man. He wants to do well for the country, and any hint of scandal could ruin his chances. I'm asking you to tell me what the problem is so I can head it off."

Deacon was silent for about two floors then said, "You have time for lunch?"

We went to a subway down from the Wynn Towers and ordered. We got our orders, went outside and sat in the shade of one of the entrances to the MGM Grand.

"How close are you to Macey?" Deacon asked.

"Close enough to be his personal security team leader for the last two years. I've known the man for much longer than that. He offered me the job after I left LVPD. He's a good man, Deacon. I'd hate to see anything sully his reputation."

Deacon was silent for a moment as he ate his sub. I watched Baker's face to see if he had any tells. He showed no emotion, no looks to suggest that he was hiding anything.

Deacon spoke after he polished off the sub. "Do you know about Alfred Horn or Taylor Higgs?"

"I do. I was asked by Macey to check them out, which I did. I found out a little about each, and why Higgs was harassing Macey. Horn had nothing to do with the Senator. I don't think he even knew Macey was in town."

"So you never had any contact with Horn?"

"Never met the man, just heard about him through Higgs. Higgs said that Horn knew about a scandal in Macey's past that would go away if the price was right. Macey was upset and had me investigate Higgs. I was still investigating when you showed up. That's why I'm asking."

"Did you know both Higgs and Horn are dead?"

Baker looked surprised. "No, I didn't. When?"

"Last couple days. Horn was murdered in a restaurant, and Higgs was murdered in a hospital while he was in a coma, death by poison. You don't know anything about that?"

"I said I didn't. This is all news to me." Baker sounded a little miffed.

"You wouldn't know about Horn's apartment being tossed?"

Baker was quiet for a bit too long. Deacon asked again, "You know about his apartment being tossed?"

"I don't want to incriminate myself or any of my men. What if I knew about it?"

"It would solve one thorn in this case. Did you do it?"

"I'm not saying who did it, but I may know about it."

"Just suppose someone was blackmailing Macey with damaging evidence. Wouldn't one do what they had to do to get said evidence back? Even tossing an apartment?"

"Makes sense to me, if I knew who tossed the apartment."

"Think someone may have found something?"

"If I knew about the apartment being tossed, I'd say nothing was found."

I was enjoying this banter of denial between the two of them, but it was clear Baker had someone search Horn's apartment.

"How would someone know if Horn was out of his apartment to search it?"

Pasta Murders

"Maybe someone would find out if he was in and then watch for him to leave. Simple to radio an inside man to go search."

Now I understood about the second man in the video, the one who inquired if Horn was in that night. They had him under surveillance.

Deacon smiled and said, "Okay, I still don't know who could have tossed the apartment, and I'll leave it at that. For old time's sake. But I hope you know nothing about the murders, or I'll have to forget our past."

"Deacon, I honestly know nothing, and I 'm sure Macey knows nothing. Thanks for that."

"Did you come across anything about Higgs and the Nazi party here in Vegas?" Deacon asked.

"I had men watching Higgs after his talk with Macey. He was evidently in contact with them. I have surveillance photos of Higgs outside the Nazi headquarters with two of their men. We thought we could use it against Higgs if he tried to blackmail Macey."

"Can I get a copy of that photo?" Deacon asked.

"No problem," Baker replied.

"How long has Macey been in Vegas?" I asked.

"About a week. He's here to campaign and relax. It's his first stop after announcing his candidacy for President. We're set to go to Los Angeles to stir up some star power from the Hollywood types. We didn't need this aggravation while we were here. I'm sorry to hear Higgs is dead, but it saves me a lot of headaches."

"Maybe not. We think someone has the missing files on Macey and his run-in with the Nazis," I said.

He looked at me. "We can deny what they say. All that was in those files was hearsay from people who said they saw Macey at the Nazi headquarters function. Macey's a politician. He'll wiggle out of it. About as bad as Obama's birth certificate. They're still denying that."

"You saw the files?" Deacon asked.

"I talked to people who were around back when this was all happening. They said it was sketchy about Macey's association with the Nazis. No real proof, but we wanted to be sure this would go away and Macey wasn't going to pay ransom for the files."

"Okay, I'm glad to see you're doing well. Hope the pay is good." Deacon laughed.

"A lot better than detective salary, and a lot less headaches."

We stood, and they shook hands. Baker went up the strip as Deacon and I went back to our car. Deacon stopped with his hand on the door. "Baker was a cowboy when he was on the force. He had to do things his way, which is why he left. Too many restrictions."

"When was this?" I asked.

"Just after I moved here to live with Lynn. You were still out in Michigan, and Baker was in our squad. I worked with him for almost six months before he left. Warren moved into his detective slot. It's been a smoother running team now. Not that I didn't like Baker, but I can see him and his men breaking into Horn's apartment. He did things his way."

"Well, we've spent the better part of a day with all this. We now know who was in Horn's apartment, and I don't think Baker had anything to do with Horn's murder. It had to be a separate crime from the missing file fiasco."

"I agree. Now who wanted to murder Horn? We need to get our heads back to the beginning and start fresh. Let's call it a day and get some rest."

"I'm all for that," I said, "I need to see what my two girls are up to. Probably out spending money at the mall." My cell phone buzzed. I answered and listened.

"Mr. Richards, this is Jerry from Tomkins Moving. We've got all your stuff in your storage."

*

Chapter 27

I was surprised that they had finished in such a short time. I hoped they didn't just toss everything in boxes and throw them around. Not that there was anything I would be upset about. It wasn't my stuff, and I was probably going to throw out most of it anyway.

"Thank you, Jerry. I appreciate the call. Did you get a couple locks from the office to put on the units?" I asked.

"Yes, sir. I left the keys with the manager. I'll send you the bill tomorrow."

I thanked him again and hung up.

"Well, all of Higgs' and Horn's property is secured in my storage units. We can go through the things at our leisure," I said to Deacon as we drove out of the parking structure.

"Not that there's anything there that we haven't already looked through," he replied.

"I think there will be a number of furnishings that Carol will like. Horn and Higgs both had a flair for decorating."

"Because they were gay?" Deacon smiled.

"It helped, but they had good taste, too."

"I'm not crazy about going through all that again. We didn't find anything the first two times. I doubt we'll find anything looking again."

"Well, I'll be going through it again to get rid of most of it. I'll let you know if I find anything," I said with a smile.

We pulled into the precinct, and I thanked Deacon for the fun afternoon with a politician.

"Jim, I know you don't like politicians, but thanks for being there. When you're around, I feel better."

"No problem. I'll call you later, and we can confer on the case." I laughed and went to my car.

I arrived at our happy little home and parked. I didn't find the girls in the house, so I figured they were in the pool. I was right. Willy was swimming between the two of them as they frolicked. Now's there's a word I haven't used in a while, frolicked. I'd have to include that in one of my books.

Pasta Murders

I went to the plastic chairs and sat until Carol spotted me. "Come on, in the water's fine." She beamed.

Penny pulled up to the edge of the pool and said to Carol, "He's not fond of water. So don't waste your breath."

"I'm not fond of drowning. They'd probably find my body floating in the pool one day."

"Did you catch the killers yet?" Penny asked.

"No, but we solved a few things. Oh, and I have some furnishings for an apartment for Carol."

"An apartment? I'd love that," Carol said.

"Why can't she stay here?" Penny asked.

"Because she needs her own space, and so I don't worry when she comes home late at night or wants to bring a male friend over." I smiled, then said to her, "I'm not going to hover over you, Carol, and I think an apartment would be good for you."

"Okay, I guess that would be better, Dad," Penny said with a laugh. "Now where are all these furnishings?"

"In a couple storage units. We can go there if you'd like to rummage. It's all used stuff, from two apartments that were abandoned."

"Abandoned how?" Penny asked.

"Don't ask." I smiled. "I have a lot of good stuff, and it's free, so don't question where it came from."

Penny gave me the evil eye and then took Carol in the house. I wondered just when she would get in my face about being so secretive. I knew I would have an interesting night.

The girls dried off and dressed, then we all piled into the Crown Vic and drove over to the storage place. I keyed in the gate code and went to the office to get the keys. I found the units, side by side to make it easier to explore, and got out of the car. The women followed me to the first unit as I unlocked it and started to roll up the door.

"I had a moving company haul this stuff here so I don't know if they packed it very well," I said as I finished pulling up the door. I was surprised. Everything looked well packed and carefully stacked in boxes. I went to the first pile and opened the top one. It contained kitchen things. The women were going through the other boxes like it was Christmas. I found the furniture in the back and called Carol to come and see what she might want.

"Whatever you'd like to keep, let me know. The rest will be sold or thrown out," I said as I surveyed the area. This was Higgs' stuff. I could tell by the couch.

We spent about an hour going through the boxes. There were some personal things like toiletries that I told the women to ignore. Some boxes had clothes, surprisingly a lot of women's clothing. I realized that being gay, Higgs could have indulged in cross-dressing.

Carol and Penny drooled over the clothing, all nicely hung on a rack that must have been in the apartment. They held dresses up and compared fashions.

"Jim, who did all these great clothes belong to?" Penny asked.

Pasta Murders

"Someone who no longer needs them," I replied.

She came over to me and said quietly, "You've been very mysterious about this stuff. Now talk or I'll cut you off from sex for a month."

I hesitated and called Carol over to save the trouble of explaining twice. She came, and I started the story, trying to make it short.

"Okay, this stuff was left at the Boulevard Towers, that fancy and expensive apartment complex."

"Yes, it's very high class and full of rich people. This was left there?" Penny asked.

"It was, because the owners were both murdered," I said quickly.

"Murdered? This stuff belonged to dead people?" Penny gave me a look. One that I should cringe at, but didn't.

"Yes." I was ready to duck, but she actually smiled and turned to Carol.

"Does that bother you?" she asked.

Carol smiled, too, and said, "No, there are some nice things here. Besides I'm used to having second hand furniture from back when Mom used to have to move around. We furnished a number of places from Goodwill. Probably most of that stuff was from dead people."

"Okay, if you don't mind, I'm good with it," Penny said. She gave me a smile, but I figured that later she might ask more questions. We finished Higgs' things and went on to Horn's. I closed up Higgs' unit and opened Horn's. It was packed just as well as the other. I'd have to recommend the movers.

Bob Moats

We went through the boxes, and Carol said she liked the furnishings in there better. I was digging through a box when I heard Carol let out a little squeal. I jumped and went back to her, figuring she found a mouse. She was standing holding the Remington typewriter that Horn had for years.

"I love this! It's an old typewriter, the kind of thing they used before computers," she said, looking very happy.

"Well, it's yours if you want it," I said. I'd hoped to keep that one myself, but she looked so happy, I couldn't take it now. "It's gone through a couple wars and was used to type up many government documents, including secret ones. You're holding a piece of history there. I'll tell you more about it later."

I watched as she went to set it on a table but tripped on a stool sitting below her. The typewriter dropped to the concrete and broke open in two pieces. She gave a small cry as it hit. I went to help pick it up.

"Damn, look what I did." She was almost in tears.

"Hey, it can be fixed. These things are indestructible. Well, they do come apart if dropped." I smiled to relieve her.

"I feel so bad," she said as I picked up the base of the thing and put it on the table. I lifted the rest and was surprised to see a book stuck in the bottom of the thing. It couldn't be seen with the base on, but there it was. Horn's Moleskin journal that was missing.

Pasta Murders

I jumped up and kissed Carol on the cheek. "You may have just helped to solve my case, if this is what I think it is."

She looked surprised as Penny came over to see what the noise was. I held the book up and said, "This is a missing book Horn owned that he used to write in. Remember at the restaurant?"

"Sure, the one we thought he was writing about Angelo's review," she replied.

I opened it and read a few pages. I was startled by what I read. I turned to the last few pages he wrote in and smiled. "I need to call Deacon." I went out of the unit, pulling my cell phone from my pocket.

About twenty minutes later, Deacon drove in while I was reading more of the book. It contained information about many well-known persons, some of it potentially embarrassing to those people. It also contained information on Horn's last night and what took him to Angelo's.

"Talk to me," he said as he came into the unit. I was sitting on an easy chair that I had pulled out from the pile of furnishings.

I smiled and said, "Pull up a chair. Have I got a story for you."

*

Chapter 28

I sat reading things from the notebook, while Deacon was soaking it up. Penny and Carol came out and stood listening as I read out loud. The passages involved kickbacks and bribes he had received from prominent restaurants and owners of the casinos for good reviews.

"Too bad Angelo didn't use his mob connections to bribe his ass," Penny said with a laugh.

"This is a journal of all kinds of bribes and payoffs, and a little blackmail thrown in to boot. Horn wasn't a very nice man. The last few pages detail his reaction to Angelo's restaurant, but it says that Horn didn't want to get involved with Angelo because of his mob connections. He was afraid of the Traviano family. He knew of them from time spent in New York."

Deacon was getting impatient. "So who lured Horn out of his apartment and to the restaurant?"

"That, my friend, is something I'll reveal when we go to Angelo's tonight. I called him while waiting for you to get here. After he closes at eleven, I asked him to have all his employees stay. I'm going to do this old style, reveal the killer like they did in the movie Clue."

"That movie had about five endings," Carol said.

"You mean, like Inspector Clouseau reveals his cases?" Penny laughed.

Pasta Murders

"Hey, I have the culprit. I want to have my fun. Now let's close up here and go to Momma Mia for some late night fun."

Deacon peeked into the unit and said, "Glad I didn't have to go through this mess."

I closed the door and locked it, herding everyone to the cars.

We drove to the restaurant and parked. I led everyone in, and we went to the side dining room as Angelo came up.

"So, Mr. R, you have found out who was the killer?" he asked.

"I do believe I have, my friend. Now is everyone here that I asked to be here?"

"Yep, I made sure to tell everyone to stay for a meeting about the restaurant. They all agreed. We have about fifteen minutes before we close. Would you like a drink, on me?" He grinned.

I was feeling good, so I asked for a beer. One for me and one for Penny. I looked at Carol and said, "You can't drink. You're the designated driver."

She laughed and said it was fine with her.

The restaurant closed, and all the customers left. We waited until the staff had the tables cleaned and the place was ready for the morning opening. I sat patiently waiting, but Penny was ready to kill me to get the answer to the murder. I held her off the best I could.

Finally Angelo called in all the employees to sit by us. I stood and went to the head of the group. I was feeling smug, but decided maybe I should pull it back a little. I did.

Bob Moats

"You are all here because you know that a murder was committed here the other day. We have found evidence that suggests one of you murdered Albert Horn. I have his personal journal, the one he kept meticulous notes in. He explained in detail about his evening here at the restaurant." I looked at Angelo. "It was all good, despite his harsh actions towards the employees. He had to see if you all could hold your tempers. You passed with flying colors."

Everyone let out a little cheer as I continued. "But there was one person who wasn't happy to see Horn here, and he called Horn at his apartment and lured him back here under a false pretense." I wondered if I sounded like one of those detectives in the movies revealing the killer. I looked around at the people seated before me, all looking calm and collected except one.

He stood behind Penny and Carol and tried to avoid looking at me. I wanted to end this so I opened the book and read, "Received a call from someone at the restaurant I just left saying that I should come back to discuss a matter of extreme importance. It had to do with a past column of mine involving someone who committed suicide. I knew why he did it, and I was responsible for his death. I asked who the caller was, and he said to come or he would reveal what he knew about the suspicious death. I was intrigued, so I sent my review to the paper," I looked at Angelo, "and went back out."

"That was all he wrote. I presume he hid the book in the typewriter in case it would be needed. We'll never know his motives now. But he was killed here by one of you." I looked straight at Harvey Rush, the manager of the night shift. He turned away.

"Harvey, will you tell us why you killed Horn?" I requested solemnly.

Harvey turned and yelled, "Horn killed my brother! That bastard wrote horrible things about him in his column, about my brother's restaurant. It closed down after that bad review. My brother put his life and all his money into that place. He was devastated, and I blame Horn. Horn knew he was the reason that my brother killed himself, but he didn't want to admit it. I brought Horn here to make him confess to responsibility for my brother's death. I made him eat the same pasta that he called Italian scum in his column. I fed him like he deserved to eat, feeding his fat face. I couldn't take it anymore, so I came up behind him and strangled him with the garrote. Is that what you want? I don't care, I got my revenge. But you'll never take me in," he said.

Deacon moved toward Harvey.

I hadn't thought about it, but he was behind Carol. He grabbed her, pulling her up and holding a knife to her throat. I was gripped with panic. I didn't want to lose the daughter I never knew I had. Penny was on her feet beside me. Deacon had his gun out as I pulled my Glock and pointed it at Rush. "Let her go, Harvey. You won't get out of here alive."

"If I don't leave alive, she won't leave alive!" he screamed. He tightened the knife to her throat as she made a painful noise. I wanted to shoot but I wasn't that good of a shot. Deacon was worse than I was. As long as Harvey was behind Carol, he was safe. Then I thought about Penny. I looked at her just as she raised her .38 and took one shot, bringing Rush to his knees, screaming in pain. She'd hit his shoulder on the side holding the knife. I knew from past cases when Penny shot someone, she never missed. She had nerves of steel and could plug a spider on the wall.

Deacon rushed over and grabbed Harvey's other arm as a number of uniforms came rushing in. Deacon had called for backup as soon as we arrived. They'd waited outside until we needed them. Like now.

Deacon called for an ambulance, and the EMTs took Harvey to get him patched up then transferred to a nice warm cell for the night.

Deacon came over to Penny and me as we were comforting Carol who was having a minor breakdown. She had never been involved in such a situation.

"Penny, Lynn has said it before, if you ever want to join LVMPD, let us know. We need sharpshooters like you."

"I'll think about it, but I'm happy where I am," she said with a grin.

I kissed her cheek and said, "You're my sharpshooter."

She gave me her evil little smile and said, "Yes, and you better never forget it."

Carol looked up and said with a sigh, "I thought I was a goner there."

"You have to get used to our lifestyle and Penny's ability to aim a gun," I said with a smile.

"Thank you, Penny. I owe you my life."

187

Pasta Murders

"No one owes me anything. It's all part of the P.I. life. Shall we get out of here?"

Angelo came up and said, "Mrs. R, if you want, I could give you job as an enforcer here."

"Thank you, Angelo, but as I told Deacon, I'm happy where I am."

"Angelo, you need to screen your employees better," I said with a laugh.

"I will Mr. R. Maybe I'll have the family do the background check from now on."

We left the restaurant and went back to the house. "So you found out who killed Horn. What about Higgs?" Penny asked as we pulled into the drive.

"Yep, that's still a mystery. But we will solve that, also. Time will tell." Carol went to her guesthouse, and Penny and I went in to calm Willy who was running wildly around in the kitchen. "Damn dog, you'd think you were starved." I poured him his kibble, and he attacked it.

Penny came up behind me and whispered in my ear, "You were good tonight, playing the part of the famous detective revealing the criminal. I was impressed."

"It wasn't much. If I hadn't found the book, I would have never known."

"Yes, but the book never mentioned Harvey's name. How did you know?"

"Ah, that's the reason detectives bring all the suspects back to one room. They watch the reactions of the people and deduce who the guilty party is. I had no idea in the beginning, but everyone was so calm except Rush. I figured he had to be the one."

"Clever."

"Classic deduction. Like in the old Thin Man movies. He always had the group gather so he could ferret out the killer."

She patted my beer belly and said, "You aren't exactly the Thin Man, but I wouldn't trade you for him."

*

Chapter 29

The next morning I was standing at the front window, toast in one hand, orange juice in the other, looking out as Carol waved then got into her car and drove off to work. She had calmed down after we got back last night, and everything was good in the world.

Penny snuck up behind me and just about made me jump out of my skin.

"That's for keeping me in the dark about who the killer was." She laughed.

"I wasn't sure, so I couldn't say until everyone got together. Are you taking Willy today?"

"Sure, he can go play with my make-up people. Are you going after Higgs' killer now?"

"We'll see if Deacon wants to go to the trouble. Horn was our money shot. If we hadn't solved his murder there would be hell to pay from Weber. Higgs

189

was just a low life pimp for gay men and a blackmailer to boot. No one will mourn his passing."

"Whatever. You don't need killers running loose in the city. Bring them to justice, and world peace will follow."

I watched her get her oatmeal ready and fell more in love with this woman. Willy came up and jumped on my leg. "Haven't you been fed yet?" I said, knowing he hadn't. I was the one who fed him. I poured him a bowl of his treats, and he attacked them.

About a half hour later, I was ready to go fight crime, and Penny took Willy off to the studio. I went to the Crown Vic and drove to my office. I had been neglecting to show my face to let everyone know I was still alive. I parked and went in to say good morning to Tracey, then went through the glass doors to Lacey's domain. She looked up in surprise.

"Now what did I do?" I asked.

"Nothing. Just happy to see you. Earl wanted to see you, also, when you came in."

"Thank you," I said and went to his office. He was seated at his desk with the phone pressed to his ear. He waved me in, and I sat. After a few minutes of listening, he said good-bye and hung up.

"Jim, have you talked to Harold lately?" he asked.

"Not since the other day, why?"

"He called and said he had some intel for you on Macey. He couldn't get your cell number to work."

I pulled out my cell phone and saw it was turned off. I never turned off my phone, but that had happened before. I think I do it in my sleep so as not to be disturbed. I turned it back on and had a voice mail. I presumed it was from Harold. I listened, and it was, so I excused myself from Earl and went to my office.

"Harold, sorry, my phone was shut off. What can I do for you?"

"I hear you and your cop friend stirred up the Senator. He's now giving details to the media about his relationship with the Nazi party from several years ago. Smart move, get there before the enemy drops the bomb. I hear you have a suspect for Horn's demise."

"He confessed in front of about ten people and tried to take a hostage. Penny shot him, and he's cooling in a cell."

"Penny seems to save the day a lot." Harold laughed. "Maybe you should practice more with your weapon."

"I'll never be as good as she is. But don't tell her that."

"Well, I'm glad you solved Horn's murder. Had nothing to do with the documents, eh?"

"No, it was a person out for revenge for his brother's death. Horn was responsible for that man's suicide. We don't know about Higgs' death yet, so the case is still open."

"Well, I'd look to your Nazi buddies for that. Just saying." I could tell he was smiling, that he had something he wasn't sharing with me. He hung up.

"Damn it, Harold!" I yelled into the phone after he was gone. Then I called Deacon.

"How's Rush doing?" I asked when he answered.

"Quiet for the night. I'm waiting for his lawyer to arrive. He asked for him. I'm not holding my breath. We have ten witnesses to his confession to murder and to threatening Carol. So he's going to go away for a long time.

"I got another cryptic message from Harold about Higgs and his association with the Nazis. Did you ever get that picture from Baker?"

"As a matter of fact it was delivered this morning with about four others, all showing Higgs with the storm troopers. I think one of them is Reese, but I have his wife coming in to identify his body and the photo."

"I'll stop by soon after I see that things are running smoothly here in the office."

"You mean that you'll have Lacey see everything is running smoothly." He laughed and hung up.

"Yeah, that, too," I said, speaking into the dead call.

I went back out to the lobby and stood looking at Lacey as she pored over her paperwork. She glanced up and jumped when she saw me. "You just love scaring me, don't you?"

"If you didn't get so involved in your work, you'd see people around you. I'm leaving, so rest easy now."

"Good, just call before you come back," she yelled.

"I will!" I yelled back, smiling as I left the building.

Bob Moats

I drove over to LVMPD and parked. The same desk sergeant was stationed at the back entrance. He gave me the same smile as before, and I wondered about him. I arrived at Lynn's office to find Deacon standing outside the office talking to Mrs. Reese. I came up, and Deacon smiled.

"Jim, you remember Mrs. Reese?"

"Yes, I do. How are you today?" I asked.

"Not great, but better than the other day." She must have remembered me.

Deacon said, "I'll take you to where your husband's body is located, but first I need you to look at some photos." He took her in the office and asked her to sit. I came up behind and stood by the door.

Deacon spread the five photos before her and asked, "Can you tell me if your husband is in any of these pictures and possibly who the other people are?"

She looked through the photos and identified her husband in three of the five. "The other men are in the group of idiots who make up this Nazi gang of thugs."

"Thugs?" Deacon asked.

"Louis and the rest of them were out to get rid of people they felt didn't fit their doctrine of hate. I told Louis to be careful, but he was a mean man. The night he left to go talk to Higgs, he said he'd be back soon. He never came back. I assumed he was in jail for killing Higgs, but you told me he was already dead when Higgs was murdered. I'm not surprised. If Higgs murdered him, you can bet the rest of the gang murdered Higgs."

Pasta Murders

"They went to a lot of trouble fixing Higgs' car to crash then poisoning him in the hospital. Why?" I asked.

She looked at me. "They didn't want to bring attention to their group. They said it wouldn't be wise. I heard Louis say that many times. They had to be stealthy about their crimes. I can assure you they had something to do with Higgs' death."

"Thank you, Mrs. Reese. I'll have an officer take you to the morgue so you can identify the body." Deacon called for a uniform, and he took the woman out.

"It makes sense," I said, taking a seat. "Reese goes to kill Higgs, Higgs kills Reese, the rest of the Gestapo boys kill Higgs, but quietly, so not to bring attention to them."

"That's my thought, but I don't want to pursue it. I'm calling my buddy in the gang unit and giving him all the facts. They're better equipped to handle something like this. As far as I'm concerned, the case is closed." Deacon smiled as he sat back.

"Macey has covered his butt by coming out with the info on his past, the Feds will probably give up looking for the missing files, and whoever has the files will find them useless now. Looks like a win for the Senator," I said.

"I never liked the man, but I'm glad he can go on without scandal," Deacon said.

"How's Lynn holding up?"

"She's actually enjoying her bed stay. She's been watching TV too much, all those talk shows. I have to listen to her explaining about all the terrible things people do. I don't care what man is sleeping with which sister of his wife. Don't these people have any morals?"

"Nope, and I don't care, either," I said with a grin. "I guess I'll go home. Oh, have you heard anything about the DNA tests?"

"Larry in the forensic lab said they'd rush it and call when ready. It may look cool on TV that they can run those tests and come up with an answer in five minutes, but it doesn't work that way in real life. I'll call you when they're ready."

"Thanks. Say hi to Lynn for me." I stood, and we said our good-byes. I went to my car and sat for a while thinking about what to do now. I should go to the office in case someone came in looking for a P.I., but that would mean work. I'd let Trapper or Earl handle it. They had more energy.

I really needed to start taking vitamins.

*

Chapter 30

I drove to my office and went in the back way, setting off the cowbell. I waved to the security camera and went to my office. I was sitting at my desk when I felt a tug at my pant leg. It was Willy. I was surprised to see him, knowing Penny took him to work with her that morning. I had my answer when Penny came into my office.

Pasta Murders

"Thought you'd slip in unnoticed, eh?" She came over to me and sat on my desk facing me. "Shall I be your secretary and breathe heavily while I take dictation?"

"You can get off my papers, and I hope you're not sitting on the stapler," I replied, trying not to smile.

"Spoil sport. I have some news. Angelo called me and said he'd like to send Carol to the Las Vegas School of Culinary Arts to train as a gourmet chef."

"Wow, that's good. I'll cover the tuition to make it easier for Angelo."

"I figured you would. I've always said you love giving away your money. That's why I'm saving every dime I make because when you kick off you'll leave me with nothing."

"Nonsense, you know very well my insurance policy will make you a rich woman many times over."

"Yes, I know. Shall we go home and I'll give you an extremely rough bout of sex guaranteed to make your heart explode?"

"My heart will explode if I try to push you off my desk."

She gave me a scowl and stuck her tongue out then got up and went to the door turning back with a wicked grin. "My offer is good only for the next hour." She giggled and left.

What the hell, I thought and followed her out of the room.

~~*~~

Four days later I was in my office when Penny and Carol came in. It looked like they were going to gang up on me.

"To what do I owe this unexpected pleasure?" I asked.

"I thought you'd know. Deacon called me and said to bring Carol to your office. Didn't he call you?" Penny asked.

"No, he didn't," I said as I pulled my cell phone out of my pocket. Damn, it was shut off again. I flicked it on and waited for it to boot up. I had moved the thing farther from my bed so I wouldn't turn it off in my sleep, but apparently not far enough. I had noticed that I hadn't had any calls that morning.

"I wonder what he's up to," I said. The words were barely out of my mouth when Lacey buzzed me to announce that Deacon was on his way to my office. He came in shortly after, holding a large manila envelope. I had a feeling I knew what it was.

I could see Penny and Carol eyeing the envelope also. Carol had an expression of anxiety and Penny was just wide-eyed. This would be the end of it all. The final answer to Carol's years of wondering who her father was. If it was the DNA test results. But I figured it was since Deacon had called Penny and Carol to come in.

"Jim you really need a new phone," he said with a smile. "I wanted to tell you the Gang Unit gathered all the Nazis in that club, and they managed to get one to weasel out the others who murdered Higgs. They even found evidence of the poison that was used. So the case is completely closed now," he said and then held up the envelope. "I also have something you want. The results of the test. It's sealed for your eyes only." He set it on my desk amid the mess of papers and files. I sat looking at it, not knowing what to do.

"Everyone, have a seat. This is a solemn occasion," I said as I lifted the envelope. I turned it over and over, wanting to open it and learn the answer, but not wanting to at the same time. Finally I set it back down on my desk, hit the intercom and told Lacey to come to my office. We waited until she came to the door. "What do you need?" she asked.

Everyone looked at her as I said, "I don't want to be disturbed for the next hour. Thank you."

"You could have told me that over the intercom," she replied.

"I know, but I wanted to see your smiling face."

"I sometimes worry about you," she said and went out.

I stood, went around my desk and sat on the corner, facing Carol. "This is the answer to your years of wondering. Do you really, really need to know if I'm your father or not?"

She sat quietly for a moment, thinking. Then she smiled and said, "I kind of like having you for my father. I can get used to it, unless you really need to know."

I stood, picked up the envelope and looked at Deacon. "This is the only copy?"

He nodded and said, "It's the only one they made."

Bob Moats

I walked around my desk to the corner of the room, flipped on my paper shredder and fed the envelope into its munching jaws. Everyone gasped as the last of it made its way into mulch. I came back to Carol who was looking totally surprised.

I took her hand and pulled her up, giving her a hug then saying, "I don't need a test. I'm glad to have you as my daughter."

She broke down in tears and hugged me tighter. "Thanks, Dad," she whispered in my ear.

I broke away and said, "I need everyone out of my office while I talk to Penny. Thanks."

Deacon and Carol went out and Penny came to me. "That was a nice thing to do. If you hadn't been her real father she would be so alone. But did you have to shred the thing?"

"Who said I shredded it?" I smiled and went around my desk to pick up a manila envelope from the floor. "After forty years of being a magician, I learned how to do a basic envelope switch. Lacey was my distraction while I switched the envelopes."

I smiled widely as I opened the envelope, peeked in, then closed it. Penny was bouncing. "What does it say?"

"Does it matter? I have a daughter now," I said with a smile.

THE END!

~~*~~

199

Pasta Murders

For every ending, there's a new beginning.

Enjoy a preview of the next book, "Talent Show Murders"

Chapter 1

A couple weeks after the dust had settled from the murder of the restaurant critic in Angelo's new restaurant, my new daughter, Carol, was starting to settle into her own apartment using the furnishings from the murdered victims. She didn't care, the furniture was really nice and it was, above all, free. I discovered Carol was my long lost daughter after she appeared one day in the office of Richards Investigations and Security. She was the daughter of an old flame, and the timeline of her birth plus a DNA test told me she was really my daughter. I was happy.

Penny was busy helping Carol get settled in her new place. Penny loved any excuse to shop. The two of them ganged up on me and dragged me off to help get decorations for Carol's apartment. I think I now own shares in Wal-Mart for all the money I've sunk into the place.

"Why do you have to have all these pictures for the walls?" I asked as we brought in the latest stash of goodies.

Penny looked at me and said, "You can never have enough pictures on the walls."

"Okay, but where's the dogs playing poker?" I asked.

"That's in the batch we rejected," she said with a smile.

I mumbled to myself, "Amazing, there are pictures of nearly naked Greek women but no dogs?"

Penny heard me and said, "These are classics, not cheap paintings of mutts."

Willy, our toy Yorkie barked from the floor where he stood. "That's right, Willy, you tell her," I said with a laugh. "These women don't understand the importance of dogs playing poker."

"Actually that painting is a big seller. I wish I had the money it took in," my new daughter, Carol, said as she entered the room.

"That's my girl, thinking of profits over substance," I said. "How are the classes at the culinary school going?"

"Really good. Angelo is happy. I'm now getting dinners ready for customers in his restaurant. It's so much fun to create gourmet meals."

"Well, Penny and I will have to come in for one of those dinners some night soon. What are they teaching you?"

She proceeded to give me a rundown on all the foods she had learned to cook and prepare. I was lost in the fancy names they gave food. I was a simple meat and potato man, but I did enjoy a good gourmet dinner as long as I knew what I was eating.

Penny's cell phone buzzed, and she looked to the caller ID. "It's Gordy. Now what would he want?"

"Well, if you answer it, you may find out," I replied.

She clicked it on and said, "Whatcha want Gordy. It's Saturday and I'm not coming back to work." She listened then pushed the button for speakerphone. "Say that again, Gordy."

"I said that you are invited to be one of the judges at a big talent show coming soon to the MGM Grand auditorium." Gordy's voice came out of the phone so Carol and I could hear.

"Gordy, I already judged an Elvis contest, and a couple months ago I judged that Top Model contest. Both times there was a murder. I don't know if I want to go through that again."

"Penny, who'd want to murder a bunch of talented variety artists? We're talking ventriloquists, magicians, freaks, dancers and singers. Stuff like that, no biggy for anyone wanting to kill them. It's good exposure for your show, one that will involve national coverage for the contest finals." Gordy was close to pleading.

"National coverage doesn't do my show much good now. My talk show is only seen in Vegas."

"What if I told you they may take your show nationwide again? We've received a few feelers for another national show. Maybe the CW network again. Change a few things, and people all over the United States will see you again, but this time in

Vegas instead of Detroit. Much better location and lots of great celebrities to choose from. They'll all want to be on your show to be seen. You can't lose on this move."

"Don't change the subject. We can talk network moves later. I want to hear more about this talent thing."

"All you'd have to do is sit and watch different talent acts and decide who you think is the best."

"What kind of prize is there?" Penny asked.

"Two million dollars and a year-long contract to perform a headliner show at the Hilton where Barry Manilow was performing."

"Are they dumping Barry? Jim and I haven't seen him yet."

"Sorry, Barry is gone, but the talent show winner will have the second show spot after a variety of performers. But that's all beside the point. Do you want to judge or not?"

"When do you have to have a definite decision?" she asked.

"By Tuesday. The show starts next weekend. I'm surprised you haven't seen all the publicity yet."

"Jim and I haven't been watching much TV lately. We've been busy with our new daughter. I'll let you know by Tuesday morning."

"Tell me by Monday night. They'll have to have time to get someone else if you won't do it."

"All right, I let you know. See you Monday at the studio." They said their good-byes, and Penny hung up.

Pasta Murders

"I hate talent shows," I said when she put her phone away.

"You hate everything. What's wrong with talent shows?" she asked.

"I don't hate everything. I like you," I replied.

She had a smirk. "You'd better love me, or you can stay with your daughter."

"Yes, dear, I love you. I hate talent shows because in my youth when I first started doing magic, I entered a few. It was always the singers who won. They were favorites of the judges, if you know what I mean. Most of them didn't have voices that were all that great, but the judges would always award them the first prize. Talent shows are very biased towards certain people, and not necessarily towards those with real talent."

"Maybe back then you didn't have any talent," she said and kissed my nose.

"You are a mean woman," I said forcing a smile. "But I love you despite your being mean."

"I love you, too. Now let's hang these pictures. You stand back and tell me if it's straight."

"You don't want me to hang them?" I asked.

"No, you'll just smash your thumb with the hammer." She giggled and went to the wall with one of the pictures. She pounded a nail in the wall and hung the picture. I stood back and gave her my opinion of which side should move up or down. I kept it up until she finally said, "Go do something else, please. You're not helping here."

I skulked away to see what Carol was up to.

She was busy in the kitchen getting all the utensils arranged in the drawers. I stood at the door watching her. She reminded me a little of her mother except her mother was a lot more scattered when it came to arranging things. She had no organizable skills.

"So how are you doing?" I asked.

She jumped, then laughed. "I thought Lacey was exaggerating when she said you always scared her by sneaking in."

"I don't sneak, I'm just stealthy. Besides she gets too wrapped up in her work to see what's going on around her."

"I'm doing very well, thank you. Dad. That's going to be strange for a while, calling you Dad."

"Well, you can call me that when you feel comfortable. I don't mind. I phoned my son, your half-brother, and told him about you. He wants to meet you. I'll pay to have him and his family flown out to have a family reunion. You have a dad and a brother, too," I said with a grin. "Oh, and you can consider Penny to be your new mother now. We talked about it, and she has no problems with it. She wasn't sure how you'd feel about it."

"I have no problem if she doesn't. I lost my mother, and if Penny doesn't mind stepping in to fill her shoes, I don't mind."

"I'm glad to hear that," Penny said standing behind me. I turned to pull her closer. "I never was able to have children, so it's great for me to call you my daughter."

Pasta Murders

Carol came over and hugged Penny, then me. "How many girls can say they have the greatest parents in the world?"

"Let's not get all mushy here. We have more work to turn this place into a home," I said as my cell phone buzzed. I checked the caller ID. It was Buck.

I went out to the living room and answered. "Hey, Buck, what's up?"

"Jim, I just got a call from some guy saying he was in charge of some talent show. You know anything about this? He wants to hire my guards for security during the show."

"Penny was asked to judge a talent show, so it must be the same thing. What did you tell him?"

"Hell, they offered me almost twice what I would have asked for such a function. How could I turn him down? But why would they need guards?"

"I don't know. For the safety of the performers or the judges. Didn't he say why he wanted guards?" I asked.

"He was being kinda secretive about it. But he said they wanted no problems during the show, before or after. Do you think there could be any problems?"

"Buck, my friend, there can always be problems. I just hope there will be no murders, or Penny won't let me live it down."

*

Continued in the book…

Jim Richards Family of Readers

Thanks to the following people who are now part of the Jim Richards Family of Readers. They have read a book or more and enjoyed them. They all volunteered to be included in the list. If you are a fan of the books, send me your full name and you will be included in future books. Send your name to murdernovels@bobmoats.com to be added here and on the website.

* Achim Feifel * Al Norris * Alex Wheatley * Alexandra Delporte-Wilkinson * Amy Tapia * Andrea Bryan * Anne Shepherd * Arianda Sugar * Arlene Markowski * Ashley Augustus * Audra Hall * Barbara Hughes * Barbara Sammons * Barbara Schuler * Barbara Zirger * Beth Donohue Plenskofski * Betsy Childress * Beth Gibson * Bill Sandy * Bill Tornquist * Billie-jo Collie * Boni J Rychener * Carl Bishopric * Carla Lewis * Carole Henderson * Carolyn Conroy * Carolyn Riddle-Linington * Cassy Bailey * Cathie Turner * Chad Hudson * Charlotte L Duran * Cheryl L. Everett * Cindy Ackley Nunn * Cindy Valstad * Connie Bancroft * Corinne Kay O'Daniel * Dana Robbins Chuchran * Dana Wichita * Danielle Monique * Darren Heald * Dave Travers * David Wilkinson * DeAnn Jannereth * Deanna Miller * Deb Breuker Balbo * Debbie Carter * Debbie White * Deborah Fartuch * Deborah Gauze * Deborah Sullivan * Dee King * Denise Freeman * Diana Carver * Dixie Beck * Donna

Pasta Murders

Gould * Donna Thompson * Donny Minter * Doris Kight
* Eddie Moore * Eric Walters * Felicia Annette Bradfield
* Francine Menor * Gail Chesney * Georgiann Minster *
George Conner * Greg Colucci * Hayley Rankin * Harold
Garcia * Heidi Arnold * Irma Ranee Coy * Jacqueline
Moss * Jan Kimball * Janice Schneider * Janice Spoor *
Jennifer Redmond * Jessica Keown-Belous * Jim Beck *
Jo Boguslaw * Jo Turner * Joanne Marie Turner * John
Peiffer * John Wisbiski * Joseph Wauro * Joyce Stacy *
Joyce Trifiletti * Judy Franklin * Judy Travers * Judy
Padgett * Julie Heath * Junnahvee Benson * Karen Dahl *
Karen Grams * Karen Higham * Karen Kaiser * Karen
Meinburg Richwine * Karen Kirkman Parker * Karin
Hawkins * Karin Vasvari * Kathleen Donohue Roesing *
Kathleen Riddle-Wolfe * Kathy Hinds Moore * Kathy
Jones * Kathy Mitchell * Katie Benzler * Kay Burns *
Kelly Garcia * Ken Boggs * Keota Rodriguez * Kiera
Mccarthy * Kim Estes * Kitty Stolle * Kristie Sciler *
Kirsty Stanton * LaLonnie Scallen * Larry Morris *
Leann Parr * Lenora Scales * Leslie Marie Jackson *
Linda Forester * Linda Ingle Cox * Linda Kennerö *
Linda Magill * Lisa Bower * Liz Gibson * Lorraine
Wiman * Loretta Alexander * Lynda Bowles * Lynette
Lawrance * LuAnn Louttit * Manny Rothman * Marcia
Gibson DeWitt * Marie Calder * Marlene Bryan *
MaryLouise Kramp * Mary Lynn Gross * Megan Atkins *
Meghan Hyden * Melody Cannavan * Michael Carruthers
* Michael Dinkens * Michael Vannoy * Michelle Burns-
Mitchell * Michelle Pilcher * Micki Potter * Mike Moats
* Mimi Baur * Myrna Hecht * Nadine Sutton * Nancy
Ellen Sayre * Natalie Quine * Neena Martin * O'Della
Wilson * Pat Pollington * Pat Rohn * Patricia Jarmon *
Patricia C Trezza * Patrick Barry * Paul Lawrance *
Peggy Davis * Phyllis Bassett * Raylene Matheny *
Rebecca Collins Besner * Renee Brumley * Reta Hanna *

Bob Moats

Reta Moats * Roberta Navarro-Harder * Sally Berneathy * Sally Hubler * Sarah Santos * Satka Nikc * Sharon E. Edwards * Sharon Mangini * Sharon McMillon * Sheena Rawl * Sherry Amstutz * Shirley Alvarez * Shirley Davies * Shirley Williams * Stacie Rowe * Stephanie Conner * Steve Cullen * Susan Haughton * Susan Hesse Adams * Susan Salomon * Suzan K Chase * Taisha Cullum * Tamara Moore * Tammy Castleberry * Tammy Lynn Wood * Ted Murphy * Terri Atkins * Terri Creech * Terry Raab * Tonia Rachael Riggs-Williams * Travis Fleury-Lopez * Twyla Gawlas * Val Brooks * Walt Munsel * Yvonne Isakson *

Thank you to all these wonderful people.

Thank you for purchasing this book. I hope you enjoy it as much as I enjoyed writing it for my faithful readers. Please feel free to email me to tell me what you thought about my stories. I love hearing from the readers. I can be reached at murdernovels@bobmoats.com thanks again!

www.ingramcontent.com/pod-product-compliance
Lightning Source LLC
Chambersburg PA
CBHW060257150626
46556CB00021B/768